Burning
Bridges

Burning Bridges

~A NOVEL~

JOHN MYERS

BURNING BRIDGES

iUniverse books may be ordered through booksellers or by contacting:

iUniverse
1663 Liberty Drive
Bloomington, IN 47403
www.iuniverse.com
1-800-Authors (1-800-288-4677)

ISBN: 978-1-5320-2770-3 (sc)
ISBN: 978-1-5320-3324-7 (hc)
ISBN: 978-1-5320-3323-0 (e)

Library of Congress Control Number: 2017914977

Print information available on the last page.

iUniverse rev. date: 04/10/2018

To those I love, here and beyond.

"This above all, to thine own self be true."

—W. Shakespeare.

PROLOGUE

The stadium stood on the land as man's great obstacle to the effluence of the setting sun. But this had not always been so. Much earlier in the day the sun had rested high above the structure, pausing to lavish its genial warmth upon the earth from the midst of a vast, cerulean sky. It had entered the very recesses of the building and had been eagerly accepted. It had spread its warmth across the plain which encircled the stadium, among the houses of man, and the population had revelled in a euphoric sense of luxury. As it began to fall, it even left a crimson promise of a lustrous day to come.

Yet as a scarlet mist began to pervade the horizon; as the brilliant reds and blues and yellows did mock battle for ownership of the western sky, and the right to be reflected in the slumbering Pacific below; and as they then joined forces, old comrades again, in order to make innocent sport of the dull, greyish-brown horizon to the east, the face of the land began to change.

Like the eastern mountains, the valley seemed to lose all semblance of colour. The bright spring greens of the trees and the deep, clay-like reds of the earth were washed aside in a flood of sterile, translucent grey. The shadow behind the stadium grew steadily larger. Sunlight disappeared entirely from within the stadium's centre, until it became a defiant, blackened crater. The nearby houses each sprouted their own individual badges of darkness, while only a few were relieved by a light turned on from within. As more people made their way homeward, and as all movement seemed to gradually fade, these tiny pockets of light began to grow more numerous. Eventually, intensified by the enveloping darkness, they evolved into an energetic but flawed reflection of the crystalline stars which rested, silver white on velvet black, in the sky out over the ocean.

As a pallid green haze drifted across the land, an almost imperceptible ring of purple light began to take form around the top of the stadium. It brightened with an excruciating slowness, finally casting into the centre a torrent of bleached yellow glare which threatened to overflow its boundaries. From outside the building it shone as a brilliant blister of light, rising high up into the darkness, and falling back to dominate the surrounding landscape as the full moon above dominated the neighbouring stars. Then, as if on some unseen signal, the people began to emerge from their houses.

Their travel had a sense of purpose, as though uncontrollably drawn towards the stadium, now glowing like the golden cup of some giant, ancient god. They came by the thousands: some from close by, others from great distances as yet seemingly untouched by the structure's all-prevailing radiance. One by one their lines filled the building. Their mass consumed every available position with the exception of a large platform at one end, which was elevated above the ground and which, somewhat remotely, seemed to be the object of their attention.

They were a restless crowd, restless as though expecting something vital to happen. Their impatience seemed to flourish, feeding upon itself and intensifying under the heat and glare of the lights. Here and there they rose and fell in sharp, vertical motions, appearing as slow-motion flares from some lost, misshapen sun. Again and again chants issued forth, strong but only vaguely discernable, and died away as offerings to some as yet unseen figure.

Suddenly blackness poured into the stadium's centre, yet even relief from the intolerable fire could do nothing to quell the group's frenzy. It exploded out of the dark in a terrible scream of anticipation. For unfathomed moments it formed itself awesome and solid and seemingly impenetrable. Then, from no perceptible source, faint, but somehow unnaturally powerful, came the slow, melancholy notes of a piano. The crowd reinforced its peal as if sensing that all its expectations were about to be realized. The music played on, one solitary note after another, like a trail of footprints in the sand leading to a distant horizon and unknown discoveries. Then the music quickened.

A column of light cracked open the darkness. It landed high up on the platform and exposed for the first time the form of a young woman. Her slim figure was dressed in a long delicate dress - perhaps white, perhaps colourless only because of the light which fell on and around her like an aura. The people before her cheered as one but she displayed no reaction. Her face, also somewhat whitened, seemed sad as though she were affected only by the music. As the music slowed for a second she gently took hold of the microphone and stand before her, closed her eyes, and began to sing.

Her voice was flowing and full: sometimes intense, sometimes mellow, but always clear and expressive. Other instruments joined her, and she worked with them as they came alive or faded away to create an emotion-charged melody. Only now had the crowd become quiet. Transfixed within their obvious adoration, they seemed unable to speak, to move, even to think, able only to drink in the experience that was given them, barely conscious of the words the young woman sang.

Her song told of a questionable love: one which seemed to thrive but which was really just a mask disguising an empty, sterile existence. Her subject recognized this fault, but as truth was only a long forgotten memory, no other concept existed, and all that could be asked for was that which was already possessed.

As she finished singing the crowd responded with a roar of abrupt applause. She faced her audience with a slightly turned head and a shy, unsure smile, like a small, first-time schoolgirl who had just been told that her new-found classmates are her friends.

CHAPTER 1

She was a picture of ambiguity as she ran along the endless stretch of beach. She seemed as much a part of her environment as the seagulls that glided soundlessly overhead, or the porpoises that occasionally bobbed their heads above the water's surface, a few yards offshore. Yet something ultimately prevented her from being assimilated into her surroundings. Someone viewing the scene might have found himself at first inexplicably unable to concentrate on the woman in particular: much like trying to focus on one certain figure in a cloud-filled sky of puffy outlines. But eventually and inevitably the reality of the image would have begun to come through.

From a distance her appearance was one of freshness and innocence. She wore only track shorts and a tank-top, and her feet which bore no shoes, and hair which fell behind her loose to her shoulders suggested an unencumbered spirit, which might be perfectly suited to her two dozen or so years. She was slender and not particularly tall, and her body looked firm and capable, the result of constant activity and long hours of working out. Her face possessed beauty, but its countenance was not a simple one. Its most obvious features were a delicately upturned nose, sparkling brown eyes and a brilliant smile which, partly due to an ever so slight over-bite, never seemed to fade. Existing alongside, however, were a fixed brow, a worldly expression and small traces of a frown line just beginning to form between her eyebrows.

The line seemed all the more evident for the glare of the setting sun into which she ran. It bathed her features, giving them the earthen-coloured tones of a clay sculpture. Her entire being seemed to drink the brilliance in: her tanned skin became richer, her dark brown hair came alive with streaks of gold, and the blues in her shorts and shirt mirrored the brightness and variety of those in the ocean beyond. Only the silver-coloured pendant around her neck seemed to reject the bright rays. It was a simple, tiny, rectangular piece on the end of a very fine chain, but it glistened furiously in the sunlight, cutting the eyes of passers-by like the glare of chrome on a hot, sunny day.

The girl jogged along, her motions smooth and effortless. She had found jogging long before it became the popular thing to do. Running, to her, had always seemed merely a natural extension of walking. Her devotion to the sport had paid off. Every run seemed to shave a little more time off the stop watch she left ticking back on her sun deck. Cramps, nausea, shortness of breath, and pulled muscles no longer troubled her no matter how hard she pushed herself. She no longer felt a dull thud in her back every time her bare feet landed on the wet sand. There was no persistent dizziness in her head, telling her that she had had enough.

She had achieved the ability to confront and triumph over the challenging without repercussion, and yet she had not yet reached the point where she could completely lose herself in her running. She was far too aware of her own actions - far too interested in what was going on around her. As a result, her movements were by no means chance occurrences. Each time she turned to study the mostly vacant summer homes on the low-lying cliffs to her right; each time she detoured from her otherwise unfaltering path in order to avoid a rock or a clump of seaweed; and each time she strayed for a few seconds to cool her feet in the ocean's waves, it was a conscious response to a comprehended need.

She had never failed to strive for the things she wanted in life. She was very stubborn in that respect. If a particular course of action managed to survive her critical scrutiny, then she tended to cling to it, considering it to be unalterable. Yet the scrutiny itself perplexed her - that hesitation before action which always seemed to be there. She was fully aware of this trait in her life, and yet was equally fully unable to move against it. In some ways she felt she should make no move at all. Her career had been fast-rising and successful. She had reached the top of her profession by virtually making no mistakes. Yet sometimes she wished she could go at something blindly, with no research, no preparation and no alternative plan, through instinct alone. Failure might result, but it would be an honest failure - perfectly balanced with a sensation of having given one's all. If the result were victory, then what a sweet success it would be. But this seemed to be against her nature: she could no more forget her planning and her organization than she could forget to click on her stopwatch before a run. Like her watch, her success was a measure of the progress of her aspirations. Yet her success seemed only to deepen the sense of imbalance that she felt.

It was at such times that her running was most important to her. As it had improved she discovered benefits that she hadn't expected. She found that she could use her jogging to unwind - to loosen up and forget life's little problems. Or she could think problems through while she jogged - everything always seemed so much clearer during a run. Perhaps it was because she didn't have the usual dozen-or-so people around her, all demanding her attention, and all seeming to be talking at her rather than to her.

At the moment, however, she ran purely for enjoyment - and

because she was bored. She was on the tail end of a two month vacation and although she had both the money and the time to go anywhere, she couldn't quite bring herself to make a move. She wasn't used to having to think up things to do, which was never a problem when she was working. And yet it was a comfortable enough boredom: she had successfully contented herself with her running, her thinking and her planning. Although she was anxious to return to work - to put her latest ideas into play - this eagerness was tempered by her reluctance to rush into anything. Everything comes in time, she thought. Besides, Leon had said that in a few month's time she would be cringing for such an opportunity to do nothing. There was work yet to be done in the city, then three or four months on the road. She wondered what she would do without Leon. However, it wasn't a problem she wished to think through, so she turned her attention to the beach ahead.

No sign of human life lay before her. Yet she knew she need only turn around to view the jogger who had just passed by. He had an exaggerated look of agony on his face, and had given the usual inter-jogger wave in a most insincere manner. She knew that if she ran back a quarter mile she would once again come upon the older couple strolling along-side the breakers who, despite the amiable smiles she offered, had tried so hard to avert their eyes from her direction. But she had no desire even to turn around, much less retrace her steps.

She loved the oceanfront when there was no one around. She had lived on the ocean for four years and each of those years, from September until June, had come home to the sleepy row of beach-front homes with its sparse, winter population. Each June, before the arrival of the summer crowds, she had left to promote the previous winter's effort. The chances to meet new people here had been few. She knew nothing of most of her neighbours. Sometimes while out running, just for fun, she would imagine that each house was the image of its owner. Each had its own unique personality and age: its own individual features. She became quite attached to most of them, and if one particular landmark happened to make way for younger blood, it was taken as a personal loss.

It was, then, the summer that she had never experienced here. She had heard about the massive invasion of vacationers that confronted the area - the parties and the drugs, the movie stars and the craziness - but she had never really witnessed it. She would miss the Pacific summer once again this year. Another month and she'd be gone. Although she was slightly curious as to what went on, she had no real desire to observe it firsthand. It was the unknown to her, and although she didn't necessarily fear it, it was a source of intimidation. She was thankful for her annual tour and looked forward to each June as an escape into something she was familiar and comfortable with.

Although privacy, or the lack of it, didn't make her steer clear of the Pacific summer, it was something she certainly valued. She demanded it in fact, looking upon it as her unquestionable right. The more that right was challenged, the harder she fought for its survival. She didn't feel she should be punished because her profession made her a target of the public eye. She refused to submit to countless interruptions by unthinking people who demanded her time, but would probably want more if they could get it. She gave them her soul for their money, why did they want more? Most of the others she knew in the business tended to give in to the pressure, considering it to be an unavoidable part of the job. She didn't believe that. She had found that she could make her life as private as she wanted just by altering her lifestyle a bit, and by sticking to her beach.

Her beach was unlike any other place she had ever been to. Here everyone was considered equal. No one was more equal - no one was put on a pedestal. Those who wished to be friendly acted friendly. Those who wished to be unsociable, like the jogger and the older couple, acted that way. Not only could they be forgiven, they could almost be envied. They felt no pressure to behave in any certain way because no pressure was placed upon them. It was the same for her: she was never bothered here. Her beach was unlike any other place because it was just like any other place, and here she was just like any other person. In this respect she had no reason to think that the summer would bring a change.

It was rather the loss of seclusion she couldn't bear the thought of. The isolation she now felt contented her, ever after being alone for most of the last two months. She reasoned it was because her job was so vastly different. She faced an unending parade of meetings to attend, appointments to be kept and decisions to be made. As long as she could immerse herself in her job - the tours and the work in the city - then it delighted and challenged her. But she needed to have her refuge at the ocean to fall back on and recharge. She liked being a little bit lonely, and found the isolation made her link herself to other things. It brought out in her extreme feelings of possession.

"Damn, my own beach!" she yelled out to the universe. She looked up and down the sand. No one had heard her, she was sure, but she felt embarrassed anyway and quickened her pace to leave, her self-consciousness behind. Why had she said that, she wondered? Perhaps it was because she could have almost anything she wanted, that she desired to possess things that never could be hers. The beach wasn't hers, but she could pretend it was. To pretend was all she needed to do. She glanced up and down again. No one was in sight, there were no distractions, so she began to look around. Her senses seemed to increase in their capacity, and everything she observed became intensified in its impact.

The sun was sinking still lower toward the horizon. In another few minutes it would begin to kiss the edge of the sea. But this section of the coastline ran east to west rather than north to south. In the past several weeks the sun had been creeping more and more northward until it now sat almost halfway over the beach before her. Summer was definitely coming. She wondered if the water had at last begun to warm up, so she drifted to the left a little, carefully selected an incoming wave and cautiously made her way through it. Still pretty cool, she thought, but not too bad. Yet she had never been in swimming the whole time she had lived there. Jellyfish, that was the reason. Floating around by the dozens, ready to sting a person. Or maybe they were Men-of-war. All she knew was if you stepped on them you hurt like blazes for days, and she was always on the lookout when she was out running. And besides, swimming in the ocean wasn't necessary in order for her to recognize its qualities. She always found plenty to marvel at from the safety of shore. She supposed the average ocean swimmer fell far short of the appreciation she had for it. She felt strangely satisfied by that last thought, and looked toward the sea in search of something special to admire.

The water seemed unusually dark to her. It swirled in a mixture of deep navy blue, almost black, and charcoal grey. Yet for depth nothing could compare with the sky above. It was an incredible colour, a royal blue so clear and unblemished that it appeared to radiate with intensity. She was uncertain if she had ever seen that colour before. After some thought she decided she hadn't. But where could it be found? Perhaps only deep in the ocean, looking up through unclouded water at the brightness of daylight. That was probably it, although she felt she would never know for sure. Bound by her earthly limitations, she would have to be satisfied with the sky before her, and enjoy it while it lasted.

Yes, the sea was very dark, but it was lined here and there with whitecaps stirred up by a steadily growing breeze. The wind was a refreshing one, yet it was also gentle, and had a lot of Pacific warmth mixed in. It came from the direction of the open sea, and helped wave after wave on its journey toward high tide. She had definitely picked the right time to go running. Another hour and there would be scarce little beach left. If she had been faced with jogging on the loose sand at the beach's edge, then she would've waited for the hard wet sand of low tide and gone running at night.

Thankfully she didn't have to face that problem. Another mile down was her turn-around point, and then it was about a half an hour back. The seagulls on the beach, however, weren't so lucky. They stood in groups by the hundreds waiting for the signal to fly off for the night. But the waves were sliding in farther and farther, and every once in a while, having grown tired of the increasingly cramped quarters, they would take off to soar in uniform throngs. One such group had just settled back onto the sand when she suddenly felt the need to open communications.

"Hi guys!" she called out. The seagulls, unconvinced of her friendliness, fluttered away in a surge of synchronized panic. Why are seagulls always so nervous, she wondered? Why can't you hand feed a seagull on your lap just like you can squirrels or chipmunks? She always wanted to know what it would be like to hold a seagull: they must be incredibly light, and yet they always looked so fat. Maybe it was impossible to get close to them. If one was raised from a chick it might be tamed, but out of its environment it probably wouldn't live very long. Still, seagulls are most likely all different, she supposed, a lot like people. And just like people, contentment would be what they need to survive.

The departing flock had taken most of the neighbouring gulls with it. Yet one still remained a few yards up the beach, lazily surveying the scene in apparent self-imposed exile. Then, after a prolonged glance in her direction, it too started up and began to fly out over the water. It flew low at first, with its wingtips just grazing the crests of the incoming waves, and appeared to be heading out to sea. But it suddenly vaulted into a high backward arc, levelled out a moment later, and began to fly beside her a little way offshore. It barely moved its wings now, but rather kept them steady as it glided into the brisk headwind. She was impressed by the seagull's form, for it hardly moved higher or lower as it compensated for the changing currents. It looked so competent and strong, and so confident in what it was doing. The seagull began to work its wings again, and moved quickly ahead. It cut sharply to the right across the beach, through the glare of the sun, and flew off high past the bordering cliffs.

She followed the path of the gull as long as she could, and then looked up the beach again. The sun now sat on the horizon like a huge, half-deflated beachball. Its rays sent a carpet of gold toward her along the wet sand between the breakers and the beach. Although almost set, it still emitted a powerful heat. As the wind died for a moment she could feel the warmth sting her face where the salt air had settled. Her skin burned and she was forced to squint through the light, but she didn't want to turn back early, so she began to use the sun to mark her direction.

It was an unusual blend of colours. Its outer edge began almost white, then farther inward turned yellow, gold and orange. It appeared to have a central point; a small speck of reddish-orange resting just on the horizon. As she studied it longer the point seemed to grow larger before her. At first she wondered at this, but as she struggled to keep her eyes focussed through the glare, she perceived the slowly evolving figure of a man making his way toward her along the sand.

CHAPTER 2

S he was no longer running now. The exact reason for stopping hadn't made itself known and that puzzled her. She stood with hands on hips, wet and slightly stooped but not terribly winded, and peered into the glare. He was still walking, moving along the sand as before. Little could be told about him. She could neither claim to have seen him before nor swear that she had never seen him. He was still such a distance away that she couldn't decide how she knew him to be a man at all. Perhaps it was his walk.

Nothing unusual confronted her, and yet she had stopped running. She could no more make sense of it than she could begin to run again. A slight shiver ran up her back as she started to feel the breeze. She had rarely been vaulted from self-control quite so abruptly or easily. It was like driving along the freeway at night, suddenly finding the car halfway off the road and remembering nothing of the interval. Not so much momentary unconsciousness as a lack of concentration. But there were no guardrails streaking toward her - no telephone poles to run into: only the water, the setting sun and the approaching man.

An involuntary shrug possessed her and was gone. I might as well walk home, she reasoned. She really wanted to run back but couldn't, and it was a fitting punishment. Her short exploration into the self had made a sacrifice of her rhythm, breathing and motivation, and she could practically hear her muscles starting to tighten. With as much disdain as she could muster she began to turn towards home, but a sideways glance at the approaching man caused her to stop once again. He was closer now - she could make out a red knapsack slung over his shoulder. He was still walking directly before the sun, not particularly fast, but with a curious steadiness. She would not, however, allow herself to be overtaken. With yet another quick shrug and one last look up the beach, she began the turn again.

Her face cooled as she placed the sun behind her, but her thoughts seemed to endure. There was a peculiar sense of intimacy with the moment. Images flitted through her mind. One was of a street. Another a hotel. Yet another a theatre. One was a restaurant with many people. Then her name and strangers and many more people, all strangers. The impressions fused then scattered, leaving her disconcerted, and forsaking her reason to futility.

"Are you all right?"

She whirled to confront the voice. Her eyes caught a thrust of light, and were forced downward. White foam appeared at her feet, then jumbled away out of reach.

"Oh, I see. You're psyching yourself up. You got sand in your eyes?"

She raised herself into the glare once again. She was directly facing the sun, squinting into its fire, using her hands as a shield, and not meeting with much success. It occurred to her that she should make an answer, but couldn't seem to think of one. Yet the fellow deserved a reply. She considered for a moment, and made motion to speak, but she heard him quietly clear his throat, and she knew that she had lost.

"Do you know of a phone nearby that I could use?"

Her face burned hot, from embarrassment or from the sun, she didn't know which. She cringed to think of his image of her and her kind. But when you stumble boarding a bus, she thought, it's sometimes best to get off at the next stop.

"I have a phone. I'll take you to it. It's just up the beach."

They turned and began to walk in the direction she had come. At last her eyes found the relief they had sought. She opened them as much as possible for the first time in what seemed like a long time, and they were cooled by the darkening sky and the strong breeze. The wind had turned to come from the south and combined with the tide to drive the breakers high up on shore, leaving barely enough room for the two of them. She knew of sections of beach, up ahead a bit, where the ocean at high tide almost touched the base of the cliffs. There only one could walk at a time.

She thought of the quiet man beside her, and realized that she hadn't yet clearly seen his face. Her curiosity started to feed. Away from the glare, she was now fully free to view him and yet didn't dare. He was probably quite put off by the way she had acted, and to turn and gawk at him was unthinkable. She decided to try to make it up to him. Nothing too involved or personal. Just some gesture to prove herself a regular person. Perhaps the phone call would be enough.

"My name is Eben Christopher", said the voice.

It caught her off-guard and struck her as somewhat peculiar. How odd, she thought. The tone of it. It was stated so matter-of-factly it almost seemed to bear outright indifference, like he felt obligated or something. No, more than that. As if it was pure reaction, without thought, like reciting one's Zip Code or Social Security Number.

"And you are...?"

The words dug into her stomach and held fast. She felt her guard rising and a cloud of apprehension overcame her. Was he joking? Was he just being formal? If so, she didn't see the point. It seemed beyond her to comprehend it. What was this Eben's game? One by one the puzzling images returned, this time matched with faces and events. He didn't seem like the others, and yet how could he be different?

"Carrie. Ralston!", she replied at last. She gauged the disappointment growing within. Yet nothing seemed sure. She allowed herself a brief moment of hope, tensed for an instant, then submitted to the concern that was determined to pervade her. Her mind felt tired and numb.

"This your day off?"

It was so simple and yet so novel. Relief swept over her. She again felt the sand between her toes, caught the wind caressing her hair, heard the thud of the incoming waves. She resolved to answer something equally as refreshing. She pondered, then replied, "No, I'm on vacation."

"Oh", came the reply.

Carrie suddenly found that everything could give her pleasure. The beach, her unfinished run, everything. But what did he look like? Her desire to know was overcoming its suppression. She felt like laughing but did not. Again her thoughts were of turning and staring but she simply couldn't bear to. Girlhood crushes came to mind. She told herself that she was being silly - ridiculous even. Then she laughed inwardly. There must be a way.

She peered out of the corner of her eye, but could tell only that the red knapsack now sat squarely on both of his shoulders, instead of over one. Her eyes were definitely lacking in peripheral vision, she deduced, and made a mental note to have them checked. He wasn't walking far enough forward to see him clearly. She slowed for a second, but he slowed too, apparently intending to keep a pace constant with hers. Carrie looked ahead again, frustrated, and noticed that the beach was beginning to narrow. Within a few minutes they reached a point where Eben stepped in behind to allow her to lead to way.

To their left lay craggy brown boulders, jumbled up against the base of the cliff by countless previous high tides. The cliff itself rose dark and wind-worn, fifty or more feet above to balance a long, unbroken line of dwellings precariously on its edge. To their right the waves rolled in one by one with the last remnants occasionally washing entirely over the sand, but never more than an inch or two deep. Ahead lay only a path of sand leading up to a sharp point in the coastline where it turned south.

This sucks, thought Carrie. I'm worse off than I was before. She realized her opportunity had been missed: she certainly couldn't turn around now. A wave beside her extended itself and slid back to the sea, receiving on its way an irate swipe with the tip of her bare foot. She wondered how Eben's shoes had fared in the waves, and an idea came to her. At the moment they arrived at the sharp point of beach she took the right-hander tight, wading ankle-deep into the surf and returning to the beach in behind the form of Eben.

Carrie kept her eyes averted for a while to heighten the impact of her success and to revel in the ingenuity of her plan. But when she finally looked forward she saw what she hadn't expected: that a sleeping bag adorned the top of Eben's knapsack, and that a rolled up tent occupied the bottom. Little more was left to be viewed than two jean-clad legs, a pair of running shoes and a small Canadian flag stitched to the knapsack's upper flap.

This failure drove her to new levels of disgust. She knew so very little: he seemed tall, and had an average voice, like a thousand she had heard before. But Carrie recalled the consciousness classes Melanie had dragged her to. Her mind must have retained something. She relaxed and tried to concentrate - what had she seen? She felt him to be tall, quite tall in fact and powerfully built, with light sand coloured hair. His eyes were a clear blue, his skin very fair and his features broad - defined by a full beard and mustache which were slightly darker than his hair. He was about her age. So this was Eben. It was a relief to know him at last.

The beach had begun to widen, the cliff was now lower than it had been, and Carrie knew they were approaching her home.

She spotted the long wooden stairs leading up the incline from the beach to her sun deck. As her house came into view she started to say something, hesitated, then told Eben, "That's my place up there, where the stairs are", and she moved ahead to lead the way.

The house was one floor but looked very high from the level of the beach. It was about the size of a large ranch style, which for the area was enormous, and had cost her a fortune. It didn't look typically Southern Californian. It was done in barnboard and cedar shingles. Some of her friends had suggested stucco and red clay tiles, but she liked the house the way she had found it - it reminded her of home. The green creosote on the deck and stairs, and the greys of the house blended in with the cliff. The roof added to the illusion, for it was composed of three huge blocks which tapered at the top. Carrie always maintained some inspired giant had built a sand castle on this hill, and had topped it off with three towers for protection. Unlike the houses of her neighbours, though, she couldn't quite relate this one to herself. But then, she hadn't stopped trying.

As they reached the base of the stairs Carrie turned, quite without thought, and faced a stranger. Eben was nothing like she had supposed him to be. He wasn't that tall, probably just under six feet, slim and well-toned. His features were sharp, and his eyes were a grey of unrestricted depth. He bore the marks of long travel: beard slightly grown, beige sportshirt wrinkled, short dark hair uncombed. She couldn't have called him neat, but curiously he seemed neither messy nor unkept. This persona was centred by a relaxed, winning smile. She thought him somewhere around thirty.

Carrie returned his smile, reminded herself to speak to Melanie about consciousness classes, and mounted the stairs. As she climbed her glance moved out over her shoulder. The sun was gone, obscured by distance and by cloud, but it illuminated a silver mist that floated along the edge of the sea. They reached the sun deck and she stopped to retrieve her watch. It read seventy-eight minutes - for about six miles. God, she thought, next time I'll run backwards, and grinned to herself. In the corner of her eye Eben was leaning his knapsack against the rail, so she approached the electronic door lock and punched in the required code - this week it was Zack's birthdate. The lock clicked, she slid the door open and they went inside.

The house wasn't particularly glamorous by L.A. standards, but it was comfortable and the rooms were huge and that was what she wanted. The living room was long and low and sunken below the level of the rest of the house. It was simply furnished with taupes and light blues and walls so slightly coloured as to be almost imperceptibly blue. Large picture windows ran the length of the room and looked out on the ocean. Halfway they were interrupted by an open fireplace, then turned at the far end to encompass an antique dining set, elevated and reached by curved steps. This level ran towards the back of the building, past an enormous stereo system, and eventually turned to join the kitchen.

The stereo was where the dining area was supposed to be and visa versa, but Carrie could never get enough of the view from her house and so they were reversed for all time. The broad wall facing the windows was adorned only with a painting-a large, vibrant seascape in watercolour which she bought because it reminded her so much of her own beach. At the close end of the room by the sliding glass door there was a tiny liquor cabinet and bar, and a few more stairs which cut diagonally across the room and led up to a landing.

Carrie could still remember the awe and wonder she held for the house when she first viewed it. Leon had chosen it as an investment and had purchased it in her name without her seeing it first. But she still teased him that it was the best thing he had ever done for her. This was the first tangible evidence of her success and it had shocked her into silence and disbelief.

She turned and found Eben giving the room an odd look. It had none of the envy of her friends from back home when they had visited. He seemed to be studying the room in detail, not over-whelmed but as if determined to learn. It was the semi-detached involvement of a student who wasn't interested in the subject, but knew he must do well to pass the course. She traced his scrutiny as it travelled from the far stairs. It wound its way among couches, chairs and coffee tables, came to rest on the landing before them, and helped direct towards her an amiable smile of expectation. She returned the smile, less sincerely this time, then banished uncertainty and stepped up to the landing.

From this point one could go left, down a hall to the rest of the house; straight, through a large front hall to a courtyard and garage; or right into the kitchen. Carrie turned to the right. The kitchen was all chrome and red tile and was filled with appliances she didn't know the purpose of. That she left to Bella.

"The phone's in the corner." Carried pointed to the spot. "Would you like something to drink?"

"No. Thank you", he replied and picked up the receiver. Carrie took a bottle of water from the refrigerator, chose a cup and watched him while she poured. He had taken a scrap of paper from his pocket. Unfolded, it displayed to her writing in a strange language on one side, and what looked like a phone number on the other. Eben dialled a number and waited, and Carrie sipped her water.

"There's a phonebook in the drawer if you'd like to check it", she volunteered. For an instant he looked taken aback.

"Yes, I guess I will." But this only brought a frown to his face. Then his smile returned. "Thank you for the phone. I appreciate it", he said, and started toward the living room. Carrie followed with her cup.

"Do you want to try again?", she asked, a little too outright she thought.

"No, no one's there. I'll try again when I get to L.A.".

"And if there's still no one home?" Eben smiled once more.

"Then I keep on going. Thanks again." He walked towards the door.

"Thank you. For your help...on the beach, I mean." Eben stopped.

"It was no problem. Take care", he replied and continued out onto the deck.

Carrie stood on the landing clutching her cup and watched as

Eben swung the knapsack smoothly onto his shoulders, and started down the stairs. She tried some more water but found it unappealing. She glanced in vain at the rooms around her for something to catch her thoughts. The tiles below her feet felt cold and hard. As he disappeared from view she remembered another man, a close friend whom she had loved and lost as, in the end, he had left her forever.

"Eben!", she called out and flew through the doorway onto the sundeck. Halfway down the stairs his dark eyes turned and met hers.

"Why don't you stay?"

CHAPTER 3

Carrie bolted through the door, over the bed and into the bathroom, tearing at her sweaty clothes as she went. She wrenched the shower on and plunged under, not stopping to test the water first. Yes, this would be her in fifty years, a little old lady ecstatic at finally having wrestled someone into her parlour for tea and biscuits. But she didn't care. She turned the shower off with a squeak, lightly towelled dry and doused herself with powder. On the way back through the bedroom she threw on her favourite sweatsuit-the one in baby blue-and combed back her hair. It was only at the landing that Carrie realized she hadn't yet stopped running.

Eben wasn't far from where he'd been left, standing by the doorway with the knapsack at his feet. She wondered what he'd been doing.

"That was fast", he said.

"Pent-up energy", she replied. "C'mon." Carrie retraced her

earlier path to the kitchen. "Would you like anything special? Actually that's why I rushed. I didn't want you to lose your appetite."

"Anything's fine."

"Great. You sit. Actually I'm very glad you said that. I only know how to make one thing in the whole world and that's omelettes. But they're pretty good, or so I'm told anyway. You do like omelettes, don't you?'

"Fine."

"Great," came a reply from deep inside the refrigerator. "But from the looks of this, it's going to have to be mushroom and cheese. Normally I could write a book: 'Million And One Ways To Fix Omlettes', or something."

"Are you a writer?", he asked.

"Oh god no, I'm...."

Carrie reached the counter and set the food down. Then she looked at Eben. The movement brought his stare over from some indiscernible object in the corner. Her eyes flew downward, then to him, then back to the food.

"I don't really think I'd be much good at writing," she continued. "Well, maybe someday. Something. How about you - do you write?"

"No. Likely someday. Must be an awful pain at times. But then so's...do you need any help over there?"

"No."

"Good."

Carrie beat the eggs.

"This is a nice house," Eben declared.

"Thanks."

"Yours?"

"Yes."

"Nice."

"Thanks."

Carrie selected a pan with a slight recollection of having just repeated herself.

"You're not from around here, are you?", she asked. "I mean, are you travelling? Or something?"

"No. I mean yes. I'm travelling. Sort of."

"Far?"

"Yes."

"Where to?"

"Oh, just travelling."

Carrie poured the mixture, then realized she had forgotten to turn on the stove.

"Lived here long?", asked Eben.

"Damn!"

"What?"

"What?"

"I said, 'Lived here long'," he repeated.

"I suppose. I've lived here since I've been here, pretty well".

"That's good, I guess."

"Sure."

Grated cheese slipped casually through her fingers, adding nothing to the silence.

"You're not driving", she noted.

"Uh-uh."

"But you drive."

"I have."

"But not now."

"No, not now."

Carrie turned the omelette. It sizzled.

"You?"

"Eben...!"

She stopped as Eben started. A meek smile was sent his way, while her face flushed.

"...would you like to go out to the table? This is almost done."

He didn't leave a sound.

A flick of a few switches and the fireplace puffed into life, dim lights warmed and soft jazz floated. With a plate in one hand and a bottle of wine and glasses in the other, Carrie approached the table. A cacophonous rumble was followed by a dull thud, and for the first time she realized the surf couldn't be heard from her kitchen.

Eben stood by the long window, peering out across the sea. Down the coast sprawled a great disc of light.

"That's L.A., where the lights are," Carrie said.

He directed his vision towards the glare.

"They never go off", she continued. There's too much worry about the water to notice the wasted energy. Later, when you leave, you can head right for them, 'though you can't see them well tonight. Too much mist, well, smog. Ever been there?"

Eben took the chair that better faced the lights, not responding to the question. Carrie chose the seat that looked towards the sea. Eben glanced at the single plate.

"You're not eating", he noted.

"No. When I run I never feel like eating afterwards. It's sort of like a double benefit. But go ahead. And don't let that old thing about the cook not tasting her own food stop you." She grinned. "Besides", the cork popped, "drinking is another matter."

Carrie looked up at his face, spilling a few drops as she poured. He began to eat in a very deliberate and discriminating manner, giving no signs of being hungry. But he looked thoughtful for a moment, then gave a slight nod of his head.

"Mmmm. Oh, this is very good. You've put something in this."

She smiled at him through the bottom of her wineglass.

"You might not guess this", she answered, "but I don't get many visitors."

"No."

"Yes, really. Well, friends and some business people. But not many new people. Not here."

"Well I don't get to eat like this very often," he said, setting down his knife and fork. He took a sip of wine. "That, was delicious."

Carrie hadn't noticed how fast he had eaten.

"You know," Eben continued, "the awareness of the value of something - just basic everyday needs: food, a place to sleep, a ride along the way. You tend to forget the value until you're without. When you don't have the means yourself. Then someone appears and provides you with exactly what you need to keep you going. With no promise of reward, no ulterior motive. You'd be amazed how often it happens. Usually right when it's needed most, when you thought you couldn't hold out. I can't count the times, and I've given up trying to figure out what governs it."

He paused and sipped the wine, looked her in the eyes and continued.

"The problem for me is, what can be done in exchange?"

His eyes left her, scanned the room, and returned. Carrie felt her throat close. Was it the words or those eyes?

"Ultimately I'm left with one choice - to move on and help others when I can." He shrugged and slouched a little in his chair. "So that's what I do."

Carrie's hand reached for the bottle and refilled her glass, while her thoughts passed over the glass of her guest. She took a large gulp and leaned her head back, allowing the wine to flow freely down her throat. This latest relief was not intense. Something else was prevalent in her head. In the few moments of silence she searched her mind and found a sense of self-pity.

She looked across at Eben to find that his attention had left her, and was now sent out into the darkness towards the lights. She was alone with her puzzlement over why she should wonder about the thoughts of a man she had only just met. Perhaps such an interest would exist almost as of course, until undone by the ultimate curse of familiarity. It was a quick explanation and a poor one, and it failed to satisfy. The voice of Eben kept her from finding a better one.

"You don't like Los Angeles."

"Sure I do," came her reply. "I've lived here over four years, you know. I wouldn't want to be any place else. I love the water. And it's so quiet here. All you can hear are the...".

"But you don't like L.A.".

"Well, what's not to like?", she hedged. "The food can be good, and there are concerts. And I've done very well."

Carrie moved to pour more wine, but the attempt brought only half a glass. Eben's was not yet empty, and she vaguely remembered that it was his first.

"Oh, I suppose it's not all great," she went on, slipping her hand and its glass below the table. "Sure there's a crime problem. And bad air. Oh, and the traffic! If you're ever caught on the freeway, you'll know what I mean. But you know, I think the worst thing is the people. You'd think with all these people coming from all over the place, that the most of them would end up decent. But they don't seem to care - at least about each other."

Carrie found herself addressing her half-concealed glass. She glanced at Eben.

"But it's my work." She looked down. "My work is here."

Without waiting for an answer Carrie stood and emptied her drink, collected the dishes and drove them towards the kitchen. She reached its sanctuary within a few steps, but without the realization that there had been no reply.

Her tears fell without explanation. Certainly she deserved to be angry. She felt guilty, and embarrassed, and open. But her thoughts travelled to the other room and couldn't take hold. Nor did she wish to confront him.

Carrie dried her face with a towel, and replaced it on a hook by the phone. A vision of her last glance at Eben's face came before her for the first time. Were his eyes moist too? Her feelings heightened and she now recognized them as fear. A compulsion to defeat the fear filled her. But she could not dictate to Eben. So he would leave, and she would feel empty. Or she would plead uselessly, and feel betrayed. Or he would stay, and someday she would feel pain.

She closed her eyes and unbridled her determination. She could bring forth no image of herself asking Eben to remain. But Carrie was confident that an instinct existed which alerted one to last chances, and that her commitment would fashion her plea. Her hair tossed as she strode through the door.

As tables, chairs and wall units flashed by, she pinpointed Eben by the window and quickly adjusted her course. His image grew larger, and she sensed the re-emergence of her smile and the promise of words on her lips. She halted with a short breath when his eyes were all that was left in her vision. After what seemed like a thousand seconds, it was he who finally spoke.

"I guess I should try to phone."

Carrie was only slightly aware of Eben's walk to the desk; his search for the scrap of paper; his dialling of the phone. She noticed nothing of how he seemed to straighten and pause - how he cupped the receiver in both hands, right before he dialled. Her concern was her shock and her unanswered questions. But she found herself at his side before the first dial tone hummed.

The ringing droned on. God, she thought, how long will he wait. She hoped an hour. But this time she wasn't too close to study his face. He didn't look at her, but she knew she was seen. He smiled a comforting half-smile of resignation. Carrie breathed in deeply, but nothing came out. As the receiver was dropped into place, Eben spoke again.

"I should go."

This time panic brought life. She followed in his path to where he knelt with his knapsack, his back towards her. But her energy dwindled, and left her where she could see his whole form. There was still nothing to be said. She began to feel sick. As her shoulders relaxed and her arms dropped to her side, she was told how tense she had been. Then there came the words.

"I'll get the lights for you."

She did not know if she had spoken. She did not care if he had heard. With each step towards the doorway she felt less sure where each foot would land. But as she reached for the switch, her face caught the push of a breeze through the screen of the door. Then, as if an ebb and flow of the tide, it began to pull her forward.

She drifted out onto the deck, the wood cooled her feet, and she took gentle hold of the railing. The light through the windows gave a glow to the deck, but nothing beyond. She was suspended alone in an eternal cloud of night, where proof of the stars above could only be found in her heart. Yet she felt through her feet the deck, the cliff, the rocks and the sand below. She heard the resonance of the waves reverberating endlessly through her being.

As he approached the doorway, Eben's goodbyes were met by the touch of Carrie's hands on his, and by the sound of her voice.

"Eben, don't say anything until I'm through."

Carrie shut off her bedside lamp, and eased back onto her pillow. Silently she examined the darkness. So Eben hadn't gone. True, she would be driving him into the city tomorrow to find out why no one answered his calls. She wasn't able to put out of her mind that in one day he could be gone. But this was a chance worth taking.

Her thoughts turned to her procrastination of an hour before - how close she had come to letting him go. She tried to count the chances she had wasted, but kept losing track. Carrie smiled to herself. Like a teenager, she supposed.

Abruptly she sat up, and in a great sweeping motion pulled her pajama top over her head. She flung it away and stretched up her arms. Her naked body slid below the covers, and she felt the cool silkiness of the sheets envelop her. Gradually her thoughts dispersed as sleep came on, but she succumbed without recalling a previous time when she had similarly failed to act.

CHAPTER 4

Carrie had never eaten so much. But the food just seemed to add to the confusion. First the golden apples came sailing across the net, and she hit them back like one might expect. Then came omelettes, which shredded in the strings of her racquet. Finally there were burritos, which looked lifeless, and fell one by one at her feet. She pounced and devoured them, and the process began again.

She shook herself awake. God, she thought, I hate weird dreams. Tennis. Damn, was it Sunday yet? She rubbed her hair. Lately the weeks went by so slowly. A beautiful smell came to her notice - some type of food. As she reached for her robe it struck her that she was starving. How it was possible after all those burritos, she didn't know.

On the way to the door she hesitated, and exchanged the robe for her sweatsuit of the night before. As she padded her way down the hall, the smell grew larger. She found its source in the kitchen with Eben, and tip-toed up beside him.

"You really didn't have to" she said, and leaned forward. "What is it?".

"Souffle' a' la mer", he announced, and selected her a chair. "Usually prepared for dinner. Quite acceptable for brunch if served in smaller portions. Ever try it?".

"Making or eating?".

"Oh that's right, you're a consumer not a creator."

"Except for omelettes", she smiled.

"Except for omelettes."

He placed the creation on the table. Her first taste declared itself on her tongue, then faded to an invitation. Her eyes closed for a moment.

"You either are a chef, or should be."

Eben leaned back against the counter and gave a half-grin.

"I was, once, a long time ago. In another life."

"And I have no idea where you got the food."

"Cooking is a lot like everything - you just need a little imagination."

"Must be a million calories", she munched.

"But you've got to believe."

"Oh that's right. I'm sorry but I can't take you this morning."

"That's okay", he shrugged.

"No, I forgot I have a tennis lesson out in the valley. I don't even know why I go. I really can't stand the guy. Well, I guess I do. You see, I'm in these tournaments sometimes, and this is the guy that everybody's dying to get lessons from. There are all these people on lists just waiting. Orange juice?".

Eben stared blankly.

"So", she continued, "I get put into all the best matches. If I went to someone else, they'd put me in with a bunch of hackers. Then if I played well they'd say it was because I had no competition. Do you see what I mean?".

He started to speak, then stopped.

"Anyway, I'll be gone a couple of hours and when I get back, I'll get changed and we'll go. Sound okay?".

"I'm sure it will all work out."

Carrie guided her car along the coastal highway, south from her house. The side windows displayed a swift-moving parade of sun-bleached beige, interrupted by spots of green. As she rolled left onto the road that would take her to the freeway, she began to think. The question for her was not whether to stop Eben from continuing his journey, but how. He might contact this person in the city, but she wasn't about to let fate decide further - she wouldn't be a victim of its whims.

The car eased to the right onto the smooth concrete of the freeway. As it gained speed, so too did the continuous flip-flip sound as the tires moved along the road. Carrie knew that preparation was the key. She must have a plan - the lack of one had almost meant disaster the night before: something that would compel Eben to stay, that wouldn't alienate his friend, and that was so subtle he wouldn't suspect. Simple. But as that last thought was born there came another. Suspect what? She underwent a moment in stunned mental silence, then her attention was caught by the sight of the huge pink bubbles, just beyond the next turn-off. The Ultimate turn-off, she always called it. As she veered up the off-ramp, she was spared from noting the desperation in her thoughts.

She sped through the gates of the club as usual, not stopping to check in with the attendants. It was a little game she played, daring them to chastise her, knowing they knew she knew that they knew who she was. But as she came to a stop a sense of dread came over her that she recognized as usual also. Caught up in her thoughts, she hadn't had time to go through the ritual of preparation - the how-to list of avoiding Murray's touchy-feely tennis teaching technique. She waited until she was past the registration desk, giving it her best air of indifference, then began to rhyme off the rules. Don't be friendly - he'll only be encouraged. Ignore any suggestive comments. Avoid being feminine or sexy. And above all, don't make mistakes. You don't want to give him the chance to correct you. She reminded herself the lessons were worth the inconveniences as she reached the bubble entrance, just beyond the dressing room door. She never used the dressing room anymore. It was guaranteed they got a bigger thrill seeing her naked than she did seeing them. For sure, she felt more exposed.

Carrie entered the tube leading to the bubble and closed the door behind her. She turned and as the bubble door pulled free, a rush of musty clay dust hit her face. The door shut with a distorted clang, like she was hearing through a metal ear trumpet. She remembered that sound in the bubble didn't travel to the far end of the court. If only Murray was there, she'd have an edge. Her vision adjusted to the fluorescent lights, great discs of diffused glare floating at orderly intervals around the court. She scanned the rusty-brown surface, which she knew to be green, but which looked precisely like a moonscape except for the lines and the net. Then he was on her. She felt a shiver.

"Carrie! Hey are you looking great!" His arm scooped her up and steered her towards a sideline bench. "Let me take a look." A hand slid up her shoulder and pulled off her tennis bag. Then he stepped back. "Yeah. You spend enough time with me and they'll be lining up to get at you".

"Can we start? I'm in a bit of a hurry."

"Sure, sure, anything you want. Go ahead and warm up. By the way, I got some racquets in that I know you'll want to see. But I figure you don't like to hang around much so I got them up in my office. Or maybe I'll bring them around sometime".

Carrie turned away and began to stretch. Murray took up his usual position behind her, compelling her to constantly rotate to face him after each stretch was through. He kept up his gleeful pursuit until she was trapped against the side of the bubble, and she declared her warmup over.

They took up positions facing each other, one on each service line. From there he fired balls at her in quick succession for her to volley back. Now and again she caught the pleasure in his face as he pounded a ball at her. If she missed, it evoked a shaking of his head.

Her shots began to develop a rhythm. In between two volleys she glanced at Murray. His main claim to fame was that he had once qualified for Wimbledon, or so it was said. But it was hard to believe this stocky, aging, greyish-haired boor could ever have been a competitive player. Maybe his edge was more weight behind his shots. She smirked as she got off another backhand down the line.

The next ball caught her off-guard. It came across fast and low and into the body. She reacted and swung her racquet around to the right. Still with the backhand grip, she angled the ball away. Carrie winced. She knew what was coming.

"Car-rie! You can't doooo that!" Murray vaulted over the net. "I guess if you're ever going to learn...".

He moved in behind her and put his hands on her hips. "Square yourself to the net. Here, step back a bit." He pulled her back to him. "Start with the backhand grip for the first volley, then change grips as you go for the forehand." He took hold of her hand and swept the racquet left then right, his forearm brushing against her breast. "Now, you show me".

Do it, she told herself, and stiffly went through the motions.

"That's my girl. Now let's try one for real, hmmm?". Murray re-crossed the net. "To your forehand".

It doesn't matter, she continued. You're the one using him to get what you want. Don't let him win. Concentrate on the shot.

Carrie moved as the ball was hit. She saw it coming big and fast. Knees bent, racquet head up, grip firm, she ripped into the ball.

Carrie popped through the clubhouse door and started for her car. Might not be back for a while, she reflected. But he was only down for a few minutes, and he walked away after. She had a vision of the down-slide of her game. What the hell, she thought, it felt real good.

It started as a realization that she'd be getting home earlier than she'd expected. Now it was almost an obsession. Where had the traffic come from? She couldn't believe it was so slow. Each lane she picked seemed to resolve to be a greater model of futility than the last. Where were they all going? Weren't they aware of acid rain? Rising traffic fatalities? The condition of the nation's highways? She brushed her hair. She took off her jacket. She re-arranged her wallet. She straightened the glove box, adjusted the mirrors, dusted the dashboard and re-packed her tennis bag. She thought of noting landmarks but they were slow to come. She listened to the stereo, but each song seemed to sound a toll to mark the unending flow of her fate, from life into death and oblivion. All on that highway. Twice she caught herself eyeing the shoulder.

Then she saw the ramp. Carrie used her time to continually re-work her strategy so that, when opportunity came, the exit was hers. Her spirits flowed free as she let the long-forgotten horsepower deliver her up the wide-sweeping arc. The momentum thrust her sideways out onto the artery, wedging her between a bus and a van, and again she was stopped.

"The whole damn city must be evacuating", she cursed, and checked that she was moving towards the Pacific, and not away. More moments of delay and the sight of construction ahead, which didn't seem to be there earlier, were all she required. Out came the city map and she planned an ingenious path through the maze. She screeched to the right, leaving the weak-minded and faint of heart behind. This was one girl not afraid to travel the back streets, she declared, although she ran a number of yellows and rarely looked around. One more rolling stop and a right turn at the coastal highway and she was nearly home. Another twenty minutes wait for a left turn into her driveway, and she had gained her garage.

Carrie cut the motor, dropped back in her seat and lifted her fingers to her temple. There was sound from the dripping and hissing of fluid in the engine, but nothing else. She reached for her bag, and the door handle, and the door opened with a strange sucking sound. As she strode towards the house she hit the button to close the garage. But as the grinding and clanking ceased, so too did her steps. She had become immediately aware of a sound which seemed out of place. It took no thought to realize that it was a song coming from within the house, but that made no sense - she played music all the time. Instead, she began to listen as one does when a song is interesting, but can't really be enjoyed until heard a few times. Not until it ended did she recognize the sound of her own voice.

CHAPTER 5

O dd things were happening. Carrie was in her kitchen, but couldn't quite get herself through the swinging door. Then again, she nearly rang her own front bell a few minutes before. She was still singing in the other room and had a horrifying image of pushing into the other side only to stand face to face with herself. Maybe her stereo was too good.

When the song ended she broke into the room and lunged for the remote. She caught her breath and looked around for Eben. After a search she found him in a chair on the deck.

"You're back early. Anything wrong?"

"No. Nothing."

"You don't mind me playing some music, do you?"

"Why should I mind?", she started.

"I wasn't going to because none of them were opened, but then I saw you had dozens so...".

"It's really fine."

"You know, you have a beautiful voice."

"Thanks. I'm going to clean up."

Carrie showered and changed and stood in the living room waiting for Eben. She remembered the stereo and went to gather the albums, but found them neatly replaced minus their cellophane wrapping. She pulled out all four and stood them in order on the shelf. Alone like this, they didn't seem to amount to much. Her whole professional life could be held in one hand. Carrie always thought she kept so many copies to give to friends and business associates. Maybe there were other reasons.

She had never seen the four covers side by side. The first was of her naked, waist up from behind with arms up-raised in a shower of rays from the sun setting over the ocean. That certainly produced a lot of sales. The next showed her kneeling but superimposed over the water, so that the folds of her dress appeared to merge with the sea. This was her favourite. In the third, she looked over her shoulder amidst a background of pastel strokes, such that half of her face was lighted, half not. This was her least favourite cover. Other than the fact that it was taken in a studio, she didn't know why. The final cover was in silhouette, with a hand guiding her in a graceful twirl on a cliff overlooking the sea. She could never remember whose hand it was.

Leon would be bringing the new cover by. The record company had final say, but she felt it would pass. It was shot on the same cliff as the last one and took two days to complete. In it she appeared to be diving off the cliff into the water a hundred feet below. In reality she had dropped ten feet into a big inflated cushion.

Carrie returned the albums to their spots and it occurred to her that the song she had heard earlier was from her first album. She wondered why Eben hadn't listened to them in order, but put it out of her mind as she met him at the door.

"I guess we should go", he said uncertainly.

She led him into the courtyard and across the uneven paving

stones. There was a distinct stillness in which their footsteps echoed between the house, the garage and the high stone wall that enclosed the yard. She figured it was due to the difference between the cool sea wind on the far side of the house, and the hot traffic exhaust beyond the wall. The old, open, rod iron gate had to be replaced with a new, solid, fake marble one to keep the curious from peeking inside. It was pearl pink.

Carried hit the garage door button and stepped back to watch Eben's face as the Caribbean, definitely not 'factory', blue Lotus appeared. But he merely gave a slight smile and nodded, saying, "I'll bet you attract a lot of attention in this."

"Actually this is how you blend in. Try driving Rodeo Drive in an Econobox. Hop in."

She started and revved the motor, and began to feel strangely nervous, like she was taking a driver's test. She had to think her way through the shift into reverse, cringing at the mild grinding of gears. Damn it, don't let him think you're a stereotype. As the car glided back and she shifted to first, she let out her breath and a smile towards Eben with just a touch of triumph, realizing too late that this was stereotypical too.

She began to retrace her earlier course down the coastal road, and found herself preoccupied with trying to maximize her view of her passenger. This without turning her head, and without committing errors which would either cast dispersions on her driving ability, or reveal her interest. It was a tricky process, and it became more so as she realized he was seeing everything fresh. Apart from watching the road, and him, she started to watch what he was watching.

They glided past the houses of her neighbours, stuccoed, sun-bleached and well-tended. Each had within its high courtyard walls the closest thing to botanical paradise on earth that a lot of money and the best landscape architect could create. But the surroundings quickly changed, the price she paid for being convenient to the city. The houses became closer together until nothing at all separated them but the occasional gullies and ravines that even development couldn't extinguish. They were an odd jumble, having been built in many different times and styles, some rebuilt, some left to decay into shabbiness. It was a hodge-podge with no quaintness, seeming to bulge to the very edge of the sidewalk, overgrown with weeds. Here and there the drive was dotted with the remnants of old walls with purposes long forgotten, and patches of dirt from which a cloud of dust was constantly driven by the never-ending movement of traffic. Even the trees seemed to be impossibly bland, and Carrie felt thankful that this part of the trip was only temporary. Soon they reached the city, which had that other worldliness about it like all large centres. In daytime there was a comforting sameness as you drove past block after block of iron bar-fronted stores of vague but dubious purpose, peopled by the suspect and the unfortunate. They were all faceless, and all seemed to reappear again and again as each mile was counted off. She tried never to come through at night, when the darkness hid the misery, the neon lights shone beckoningly, and even the prostitutes had a certain unexplainable glamour. She was strangely drawn to it such that, should she pause too long, she felt she might never pull free.

On this day at least, she would face no such challenge. Only an hour later they were heading back, Eben's quest apparently at an end. His piece of paper had led them to an empty third floor walk-up in a building inhabited entirely by people speaking an unidentifiable language, who were either so confused or suspicious as to give no hint of recognition at the name he put forth, much less a forwarding address. She saw no disappointment in his face but rather a curious blankness, like an auto-matron whose program had been erased. Nothing had been said between them from the point when she guided him robotically back to the car.

Maybe he was still dazed, but she was simply unprepared. She had spent most of the last day figuring out how to keep Eben from going. To be truthful, she hadn't found a plan - she was again to rely on last chances. But it had been too easy. He had been thrown in her lap and she hadn't yet given a thought as to what to do with him once he was hers. Of course she still wanted him to stay, but somehow she felt it was no longer that simple.

Carrie swerved the Lotus to the curb and came to a halt. She jumped out and began striding across the road, deciding in the process that she needed a drink. She glanced up the highway to her house only a few hundred feet away. Maybe something to eat too. At the far curb she remembered to wait for Eben. He arrived presently looking perplexed but, thankfully, no longer dazed.

"Food?", she asked.

"I'm all yours", he replied.

She led him through a doorway which broke the long stretch of courtyard wall at the far edge of the sidewalk. Nothing suggested it was more than a garden gate except a small brass plaque to one side which read, 'Cantina Limbo'. But it opened into a tunnel, arched and white-stuccoed, sloping gradually downward to where one could see a spot of bright light at its end. They made their way along the rough tunnel floor, their footsteps echoing, until they emerged once more into the sunshine.

"This is what I call heaven," she proclaimed, "if only for a while."

They stood on a landing of sorts, carved out of the cliff, overlooking the sea. It continued back to their right through a number of glass doors, now open to the cooling early evening breeze. An L-shaped bar stood in the building which had been neatly squeezed into the space chiselled out for it. A dozen or so patrons were seated at the bar stools and at the white tables and chairs, inside and out. This overlooked a deck led to by a wooden stairway, with more white tables and chairs where no one sat. It appeared to at least partially overhang the remainder of the cliff, and was topped by a crisscross of wooden poles and sunblinds, giving it an added look of ricketiness that it really didn't require.

"Pedro!", Carrie called out and headed for the bar. "Como esta usted. Dos Margaritas por favor. Pedro, Eben. Eben, Pedro."

"Uh, buenas nochas, Pedro", offered Eben to the hulking man behind the bar.

"Peter."

"Excuse me?"

"It's Peter. Nice to meet you."

"Peter."

"Yeah, not too many African-Mexicans I don't suppose."

"Pedro. Ummm, trigame dos la epecialidad de la casa, por favor."

"Sure." He slid towards them two giant, salt-lipped goblets, glistening and green. Carrie grabbed one and headed for the stairs. Eben followed with the other. A few steps down she heard him slightly clear his throat.

"Are you sure about this?"

She halted and turned, glass cradled underhand, and sent up to him a mischievous smile. "It's not as scary as it looks," she replied and continued on.

"I'm not afraid, it's just that I have this thing about sudden painful death."

"If you expect it to be sudden then you can't possibly believe it will be all that painful," she retorted, leading him to the farthest table but one. "So sit down and relax."

She sank back in a chair and with a sigh and a sip of her drink, looked out towards the breakers. The sun burned orange through a greyish haze, and was just beginning its dive for the horizon.

"Why do you call him Pedro?"

"Well, this is a Mexican restaurant, isn't it?"

"Yes, and...?"

"So I keep telling him he ought to take Spanish but he won't, so I figure if he hears it enough, maybe he'll learn it through osmosis or something."

"I'm sure he appreciates your concern."

"Well, I'd like to see him succeed. I haven't told a lot of people about this. Peter was here when I moved in four years ago. This place has been here a lot longer. I think it started as a speakeasy during Prohibition. They used to bring liquor in off the beach."

"Must have been good climbers."

"But in the last few years the powers that be decided they didn't want him here. They tried to change the zoning but that didn't work, so they jacked the taxes sky high. He couldn't pay so...".

"So...", he repeated.

"So..., I bought it. Actually, you're the only person I've ever told. Now I lease it to him for a dollar a year. He got his restaurant and I got...."

She stopped as Peter emerged from a nearby doorway, set before them two plates heaped with food, and carried back with him her 'muchas gracias' and Eben's attention. It followed Peter among the empty tables and chairs, then turned towards Carrie.

"You got what."

"Hmmm?"

"Peter got his restaurant, and you got...?"

She paused. "I got...to name it."

Eben gave a slight nod and looked across the deck once again. After a few seconds he faced her with a raised eyebrow and she knew he had figured it out. She waited for the question she was sure would come.

"So tell me, Carrie, what exactly are you hiding from?"

"What do you mean, 'hiding'?"

"Well it's quite the buffer zone you've got set up for yourself. It might be invisible, but it's there just the same. I think it's called, 'hiding in plain sight'."

She offered a half smile and gazed out to the darkening ocean. It occurred to her he would think she was avoiding eye contact, then realized she probably was.

"You know, I'm a celebrity."

"Really."

"Yes." With that said, she at last remembered the quickly cooling food and motioned for him to begin. "Peter makes sure not to let in anyone who might make it...uncomfortable for me. I never asked him, he just does. I make sure he can."

"Would it be all that bad?"

"You don't understand." She let the tip of her fork sink slowly to her plate, and began to stare in its direction while seemingly looking right through it. "It's strange to be put on a pedestal and yet be treated like a slave. Like they own you. I guess you're an object either way."

"I would think it comes with the territory."

"All I ever wanted was to sing and afford to eat. Everything else… well, you end up believing it's what you're due, not for what you've given, but for what's been taken. You can never go back."

She picked at her plate in a moment of reflection. "The press is the worst," she continued. "They're like children – you have to pretend not to care no matter what happens, or they just go crazy. But I'm proud to say they've never got me rattled." She straightened herself in her chair and began to eat again, looking back at Eben with a grin. She contemplated him for a moment.

"So, tell me, Eben, what exactly are you running from?"

"I prefer to think it's what I'm running to."

"Just the same. Okay, what are you running 'to'?"

Eben paused with a sigh. "I don't know exactly, but I know what it's not."

"Which is?"

"The past."

"Aren't you pretty well safe from that?"

"Well, the world is round."

"So, what about your past are you trying to avoid?"

"I was an architect."

"Sounds like hell."

"I grew up in a small town in Canada you probably never heard of and I couldn't wait to get out of. I practised in the city for a few years." He paused.

"Then?"

"Then one day it no longer seemed to fit. That was about five years ago. I quit and went home for a while, then I left and I've been travelling ever since."

She propped her chin on her hand and it hid a knowing smile. "Sometime you'll have to tell me about the woman." She began to eat again.

"The woman?"

"There's always a woman."

His shoulders slumped and he looked downward for a moment in deep thought. "With such insight it's a wonder you don't write your own songs."

Carrie felt her head turn away as though hit by a painless slap. She wasn't angry. She knew how it had been meant. She turned back, feigning a smile so that he would be convinced, and began to see that the novelty of Eben was not to be a single-edged sword. She looked towards the horizon, a bank of dark clouds resting well above its line, and only then realized that the sunset could not be seen.

CHAPTER 6

The scream that awakened Carrie from deep sleep was, in its own way, comforting. As she vaulted from bed and headed down the hall, still in her pajama top and panties, she decided that either the crisis was already over, or at least its victim was out of her misery. In the kitchen she found Eben dressed only in a pair of shorts, looking somewhat sheepish, and a short, sturdy looking woman in her mid-fifties wearing the light blue uniform of a housekeeper, clutching her heart. Shared crises must give rise to common thoughts, for they both spoke at once.

"I'm sorry, I didn't expect...".

"It's okay", she replied to both of them, leaving her eyes on Eben. "Eben this is Bella, Bella...".

She was halted by a sudden thought. If this was Bella it must be Monday. A wave of horror hit her, but before she could react she heard the opening of the front hall door behind her, and a woman's voice.

"Carrie?"

She shut her eyes with a wince, then stiffly turned, giving fate her best air of nonchalance. She saw what she had expected - three figures of varying blondness, each somewhere in their thirties. The first, the shortest, was a stocky man with a neatly trimmed beard, well but casually dressed. The second, the blondest, was a shapely woman with permed hair and a very short skirt. Finally came a slender man in a T-shirt and jeans, with three day's growth of beard and sunglasses, through which he still managed to project a certain dazed quality.

"This isn't like you," the woman continued. "This is like...me!"

They faced her with distinctly different forms of incredulity: concern, shock and outright amusement. Finally it was the amused one who spoke.

"You know Carrie, it's damn cool of you to let Bella bring her boyfriends to work."

Bella retreated in a huff through the swinging door to the other room.

"Eben this is Leon, my manager, Melanie, my backup singer, and...Zack."

"Leon Speckman. I didn't catch your last name."

"Christopher," replied Eben, taking the hand offered him by Leon. Then Melanie.

"It's Melanie Black. Really pleased to meet you." Zack sauntered over.

"I head up the band, but I'm driven here by hunger."

"Carrie, we've got to talk," said Leon.

"Leon! I'm in my panties here."

"Like we haven't already looked," retorted Zack, and moved out of her swatting range to the refrigerator.

"They want us downtown," continued Leon.

"Who?"

"Hendreik and the rest."

"Why?"

"I don't know, they wouldn't go into it."

"Well then that little weasel can just..."

"Carrie you can't go," Melanie protested. "We were supposed to work on your speech for my club."

"I'm not speaking at anybody's club."

"But you've got to at least make an appearance. I promised. We need the exposure."

"You'd think," Zack broke in, "you as a member would be exposure plenty."

"I'll think about it."

"Great. We can work on a plan."

"She's not planning anything with you," Leon interrupted, "she's coming downtown with me."

"Why do I have to plan an appearance? And don't tell me what I'm doing and not doing."

"You have to plan so you don't screw up. You know, say the wrong thing, talk to the wrong people. You're her manager," she confronted Leon, "You should have taught her that."

"Give me strength," Carrie begged, and eyed Zack munching obliviously by the fridge. "And you. What do you want?"

"Nothin'. I just came 'cuz somebody said there'd be breakfast," he replied. "And to see the shit hit the fan."

Carrie slowly revolved back to where Leon and Melanie were both trying desperately to avoid meeting her gaze. "What's he talking about?" She bounced her stare back and forth between them, waiting for one to crack. Then she noticed a large envelope tucked under Leon's arm. "What's that?"

"It's nothing." Leon looked for help to Melanie, who was busy ignoring him. "I mean, it's not important."

"Give it to me."

"No, it can wait."

"I said...give...it...to...me."

Leon didn't so much relinquish the envelope, as much as Carrie took it. She pulled out a print marked 'proof', showing a photograph in which she appeared to be diving off of a cliff into water a hundred feet below. Her mouth dropped open and she thrust at Leon a look of astonishment.

"This isn't me!"

"I told you she'd notice," muttered Melanie.

"Look," Leon pleaded, "Hendreik's got this computer that generates the female figure most appealing to men between the ages of 18 to 25, a slow sales demographic for you don't forget. It really is you. It's just...another form of you."

"Yeah," interjected Zack. "This one's stacked."

Carrie discarded the print, pulled Eben by the hand from his bewildered silence, and made a break for the hallway.

"We're going shopping."

Three hours later Carrie and Eben had made good their escape. They had emerged from their cells, after donning their street clothes, to face an empty prison, the jailers having fled rather than face the wrath of the ringleader. The doors were unlocked, the walls unguarded, and the getaway car in place. It took only thirty minutes to reach their hideaway, in this case a local mall.

Carrie picked it over Rodeo Drive in order not to be seen, but paid a slight price in style in the exchange. What little light there was came from no perceptible source, giving rise to that cavern-like quality only found in mushroom farms and malls that haven't been renovated in twenty or more years, and caverns. She hoped the clothes were more current. They stopped at the food court, grabbing breakfast sandwiches in order to compensate for not having eaten. Carrie christened hers the "Cardiac Special". It was at times like this that she most relied on the edict that all food has some nutritional value. But the plan seemed to be working. She caught only a few shoppers staring, apparently unable to get past the argument that if it really was her she wouldn't be there, and since she really was there it couldn't be her. Still, better to keep moving.

So they traipsed comfortably from store to store while she bought clothes for Eben. She had been horrified to discover that his travelling wardrobe consisted of little more than two sportshirts, a sweater, jeans, jacket and a pair of shorts, and immediately resolved to fill the void. He faced each purchase with an obvious reluctance and a mild protest, followed by a quiet thank you. Carrie attributed his low-key response to an ever-increasing knowledge of her character, this leading to a realization of the futility of any resistance, rather than to any insincerity on his part. But she was by no means out of touch with his feelings. She let him carry the mountain of parcels, reasoning that this would keep his male ego intact.

Eventually Eben's carrying capacity, and the mall's selection of acceptable goods, proved themselves far short of Carrie's imagination, and it was time to go. At this point there came into play that other standard mall characteristic - its resemblance to a maze that would rival the Minotaur's. She was just beginning to wish for some thread when they stumbled upon a passageway she calculated would lead them out. It was then she realized that he hadn't spoken for a while, and wondered if she had underestimated those feelings. She placed her hand on what little part of his arm she could find to signal him to stop, then circumnavigated him until she located his face amongst the peaks and valleys of his topography. His eyes met hers.

"Eben, I don't want you to think…. I mean, I want to spend time with you until you have to go. But I don't know how long that will be. I don't want to waste it watching you wash the same two shirts over and over. If you want, you can give everything back before you leave."

Eben smiled. "I understand that. I was thinking about this morning. Will it be all right?"

"Oh, that." She started forward. "I can handle the company. They wouldn't have a company if it wasn't for me. I'll just lay low for a few days so they think they've gotten their way. Then I'll go downtown and kick their…."

Something made her halt again. It wasn't the comprehension of what he had said, but how he had said it. Or more specifically, how he had said it in relation to what he had said.

"Eben." Her hand found his arm again. "Really. It'll be all right."

"Do they always try to dictate to you?"

"Well no, but...."

"You're Carrie Ralston! I told you it was Carrie Ralston!"

Carrie recognized the intrusion not so much by the unfamiliarity of the voice, or even by the words, but by the response building on her tongue.

"Hi, how are ya. Who are ya?"

"Well, Bob and Peggy. We want to tell you that we think...."

"Bob and Peggy...?"

"Peterson. We wanted to tell you that...."

"From...?"

"Carson City, Nevada. We saw you...."

"You know, I remember you two."

"You do?"

"Sure. It was how many years ago?"

"Two."

"That's right. You were sitting back a bit."

"You saw us?"

"Sure. You'd be amazed what you can see from on stage. Hey, why don't you come see for yourselves. I'm doing a concert tomorrow night at the Edwards Centre. Tell security I said it's okay and they'll let you in backstage. Maybe we'll go out after."

"Really?"

"Sure. See you then."

Carrie whirled and made a break for it, pulling Eben with her. She waited for his response.

"You never mentioned a concert."

"There isn't one," she replied.

Out of the corner of her eye she saw him open his mouth, then close it without speaking. She would have preferred words. Instead it was she who spoke.

"Eben, you don't understand. I don't owe them anything."

"Fhoop! Hizzz."

From her years of being photographed Carrie was instantly attuned to the sound of a camera going off and resetting. But no matter how many times it happened, whether anticipated or not, it brought with it a fear and loathing that sometimes haunted her in her sleep.

"Fhoop! Hizzz."

"Little Miss Carrie, sucking up to her fans as usual."

The shiver up her back. The nausea in her stomach. But she'd die before she let him see it.

"Borland. Decaying meat nearby?"

"Oh, my sources never lie. So what is it, lackey or boy toy? Eben, is it? Got a last name or do I make one up?"

Carrie scanned the pale, stooped figure before her but she didn't know why she bothered. Borland never changed. Same green hat faded as his complexion, covering what she knew was a hairline receding well into his thin, dishwater blond hair. Same mousey blond moustache overhanging a gap-toothed smirk that never went away. Well, maybe once. Same decades-old attire which suggested he was on the golf course when he decided to abandon his conscience and take up sleazy photo-journalism, and had never paused at a clothing store from that day forward. She had never known a person who looked more like what he was.

"Fhoop! Hizzz."

"Hey! Pal! Do yourself a favour. Four figures for the story of you and Scary Carrie here. Five with pictures. Six if she's naked."

"Fhoop! Hizzz."

"National Expulsor. But she's been on the cover so much they're changing it to 'Bitch of the Week'."

Carrie felt Eben surge forward but she grabbed his arm, firmly this time. He was piled high with packages, and she knew a better way.

"New camera, Mickey?"

"You damn well know it is."

"Oh, right. I kind of broke the old one over your head."

"Yeah, well, I don't care. I'll get rich either way."

"Well good, 'cause it was worth every cent." She stepped forward. "And there's lots of other cameras."

"Fhoop! Fhoop! Fhoop fhoop fhoop! Hizzzzzz."

The flashes seemed to come from everywhere. In between the spots of light she saw dark figures scurrying around.

"Fhoop fhoop fhoop!"

"Hah! Even you ain't got that much!"

"Fhoop! Fhoop fhoop fhoop!"

Carrie couldn't see and tried to shield her eyes with her arms. She was dizzy - everything was spinning. She hoped Eben could hear her.

"Eben get me...."

She felt herself being whisked forward, enveloped from behind. She was pushed through many people and she knew a throng had gathered. Then came doors and fresh air and sunlight at her feet. She could see the blue of her car, and hear Eben's calm voice.

"We need your keys. Take your time."

She reached into her purse surrounded by shouts and scuffling and more camera shots, less noticeable against the light of day. She found the keys and felt a warm hand take them and deposit her in the passenger seat. The engine roared to life, as did engines all around.

"Just get me home", she begged.

The car bolted forward, the gears shifting quickly and smoothly through turn after turn, until it reached the high whine of a straightaway. She straightened and looked back. No cars were in sight. She turned to Eben, then closed her eyes and leaned back, her hand in her hair.

"Did I say you should be a chef?"

"Well, I did a bit of test driving, for a while."

She sighed and turned away.

"Friends of yours?", he asked.

"No. Not friends."

"Where did they all come from?"

"They travel in swarms."

She settled further into her seat and a feeling came over her like she hadn't experienced in a long time. It was as though she was little again and riding in the car with her father, late at night, when she was supposed to be sleeping on the back seat because it was past her bedtime. But instead she had slipped in her blanket onto the floor, into the darkness, where she could feel and hear the tires humming on the road. She lost herself in letting go of everything. Yet never had she felt so safe. Whatever might come, she knew he would get her safely home. But a truth came forth that she hadn't known as a child, that for everything you gain there is something you must give up.

Carrie shook herself to reality just as they reached the gates of her house. Eben drove up to the door, and she got out as he came around the car.

"I'll come back for the packages", he declared.

She overshot her amazement that the packages had been saved at all, and instead asserted, "I'm perfectly all right."

Eben gave her a long look.

"Won't they follow you here?"

She smiled.

"No, they won't come here. I contribute heavily to the County Sheriff's Benevolent Fund." Her eyes pondered her feet, then met his. "I better start working on the State Police."

They laughed and her eyes fell downward again. When she raised them they were full of tears. Her head dropped slightly and she leaned forward into his arms. They closed around her strong and gentle. She heard his voice.

"I understand."

Carrie walked alongside the breakers with Eben, bathing in the sunlight and the salt air and the sight and sound of the sea. It was like she'd been away forever. Their walk had started as a run, northward along the route she had failed to complete two days before. She had a tough time convincing Eben that it was the best thing for her, but it was he who had run into problems. Her expectations weren't high - she hadn't even started her stopwatch - but this was more than could be attributed to new jogging shoes alone. His breathing had been laboured from the start and he faltered more as they went along. By the end of a mile he could go no further. She wouldn't allow apologies, concluding simply that walking thousands of miles didn't necessarily equate to running even a few, and left it at that. But the mere act of turning back had seemed to bring relief to him, and he improved with each southward step.

Little was being said, so Carrie began to retreat into her thoughts. She pondered her hugging of Eben, or was it his hugging of her? She recalled that it hadn't lasted long, and as she once again saw the pained look on his face, realized that she had been the one to pull away. But it was also she who had been in need. And to find comfort in the arms of a handsome, caring man? That she found him attractive she didn't even try to deny to herself. It wasn't natural to have recoiled. It was beyond her.

They reached her house but she walked still further, Eben making no motion to inquire why. She felt a slight chill and looked out over the water. The sun was beginning to fade behind an offshore row of greyish clouds, well above the horizon. Swell, she thought, sunset two hours early, and felt somehow cheated. She turned her back on her disappointment and led Eben to the base of the cliff, between some ragged boulders, until it seemed there was nowhere left to go. But they approached a tall protrusion behind which was a space not visible from a distance. Carrie slipped through, followed by Eben, down a narrow tunnel which shortly opened to a doorway with a keypad. A code was entered and they travelled up a long flight of stairs, through a passageway and another door, and came out onto the deck of the Cantina Limbo.

"Welcome to Plan B", she offered. Then with an, "Oh!", she

ducked back through the door and reappeared a second later, sandals dangling from her hand. "Health Board," she shrugged, and headed for a table. It was the same table as before, still with no other patrons in sight.

Peter suddenly appeared out of nowhere carrying two margaritas, as if on some unseen and probably electronic signal. He set them down to Carrie's, "Thank you Peter".

"Peter?" He looked at her quizzically. "No 'Pedro'?" As he turned to go he promised over his shoulder, "I'll keep them coming."

Carrie grabbed at the glass and rushed it to her lips, but her anticipated thirst failed her. She took just a sip and set it down. A glance at Eben showed him staring blankly out to sea.

"Can I ask you a personal question?"

A nod of his head and she seemed to lose her nerve. She paused, then continued.

"Exactly how far have you travelled?"

"Almost around the world."

"Around the world," she repeated. "Almost?"

"Well, when I left five years ago I headed east. No particular reason - I didn't know where I was going. I just knew I had to look for a new start. I made it to the coast, then booked passage to Europe on a freighter. I kept moving through odd jobs until I got to Japan. I crossed to Vancouver, but somehow I couldn't go home. Something drew me down here."

"Your address in the city."

"No, I wasn't here to look it up. I looked it up because I was here."

"And you were a chef...?"

"In France. When you're on the road you meet a lot of people. I met this old fellow who owned a small bistro. He'd had a stroke but didn't want to give it up, even though he couldn't afford to hire anyone to take his place. I offered to work for room and board, and he taught me a lot. Eventually it got to be too much for him, his relatives took over, and it was time to move on."

"So the driving...?"

"That was in Italy. I heard of this guy who was developing a Formula 2 team on a shoestring budget. Shoestring for Formula 2, anyway. I'd done some cart racing when I was younger. I told him I'd test his cars - well, sweep up and do odd jobs, if he'd let me test his cars, and give me room and board. Then he got a driver and it was time to move on."

Carrie rolled her glass slowly back and forth between the outstretched fingers of her hands.

"Is there always a time to move on?"

Eben fixed his eyes on his own glass, firmly planted on the table before him.

"You know, one thing I've learned. A lot of people leave you in life. If you keep moving, you get to decide when."

He got up and moved from the table.

"I think I'll order us some food."

A few steps away he turned and found her with his smile.

"Don't worry. I'm coming back."

Carrie returned the smile and watched him disappear up the stairs to the bar. She swivelled in her chair towards the ocean and brought her knees up under her chin, her legs encircled in her arms. She gazed into the grey nothingness beyond, where the separation between sea and sky could no longer be found, and began to review the day. What came most to mind was Eben asking, would it be all right? Carrie knew she had faced problems before - it had always been part of the thrill. She had plenty of energy to do battle. She had full confidence in herself, and in her ability to succeed over the likes of Hendreik or Borland. But for the very first time, to the extent of her ability to perceive it, she wasn't sure she wanted to try.

CHAPTER 7

The next morning Carrie awoke to neither a scream nor a delicious smell. She pondered it as she yawned and stretched away the last remnants of sleep, and concluded at last that she had at least broken even.

The house was curiously still. Sensing no need for her immediate presence, she lingered in the shower, feeling the soft, warm water stream against her body, anticipating the day. A day filled with Eben would be nice. Maybe a long walk down the beach. They could take lunch with them, or stop at a hotdog stand on the pier, sit in the sun and talk. She felt she knew so little about him.

She stepped out of the shower and towelled dry, put on jeans and a sea-foam green sweatshirt, then went back into the bathroom to struggle through the steam and apply makeup. She took her first, bare, tentative steps into the hallway, then tiptoed toward the livingroom in keeping with the silence all around. She came upon warmth and salt air, the sound of waves, the sight of a slightly overcast day through the open door, and Leon and Melanie at the table. Both were engrossed in reading: he a trade paper and she a gossip magazine. He had his black coffee, she her orange juice, and were it not inconceivable, Carrie could swear they looked just like an old married couple.

"Where is everybody?", she asked.

"Eben went out. Bella's gone to the market. Zack said he won't come over until there's food. You just got up. . .", Melanie replied without looking up, "And Leon and I are right here."

"When will he be back?"

"Since Bella's buying groceries, maybe tomorrow."

"No. Eben."

"Oh, he said not to wait for him. There was something he had to take care of." Melanie raised her head and smiled at Carrie, then sideways at Leon, who rolled his eyes and went back to reading.

"Oh", was all Carrie could reply. She heard a note of hurt in it which couldn't have escaped the others, and which the following silence only emphasized. She quietly sidled towards the kitchen and was grateful that a half cup of coffee still remained. But after a first gulp it was forgotten. She cradled the cup in both hands, pressed it against her lower lip, and thought. Where had he gone? Why hadn't he told her, or woken her, or taken her with him? What about all their plans, well, her plans, almost bypassing the fact that they hadn't precisely been discussed. A feeling of indignity arose not necessarily justified by logic, but not needing to be. He should have known. An overwhelming desire to carry on the day without him struck her. She was getting along fine without his company four days before and could again. That's what employees were for she reasoned, and strode back to the table to find out what the morning held in store.

"Leon! Melanie! What are we doing today? I want the full agenda."

Her outburst was sufficient to draw their attention from their respective reading materials, and to turn to give each other a look like she was speaking Chinese.

"Don't everybody talk at once."

Leon looked at Melanie, Melanie looked at Leon, both turned to Carrie and it was back to square one.

"Oh come on. We've got a tour coming up. You mean there's absolutely nothing to be done? What about rehearsals?"

"They're not for another week," replied Melanie.

"What about the new release? Isn't there some work left?"

"Instrumentals are finishing in a few days," said Leon.

"This is insane! Here we are sitting like three bumps on a log. . .what do I pay you people for? There are people out there working or going to jobs, doing god knows what, but doing something!"

Both sat like wax representations of themselves and continued to stare until, at last, Melanie spoke.

"But, it was you who set the schedule."

"I set. . .?"

"Yes. You said the last three tours were nothing but, 'bullshit, bullshit, bullshit!', and it would be a cold day in hell before you'd go through that again and. . . ."

"Fine. Thank you Melanie. Just tell me this. Do we have no schedule today at all?" Melanie straightened herself in her chair.

"I'm not actually working today. I've got a luncheon meeting with my club." As the last word pronounced itself, her face brightened as if she had suddenly solved the riddle of perpetual motion.

"You! You could come along! It would be great! You could meet everyone, and everyone could meet you...."

"No! Absolutely not. I told you before I'm not going and I'm still not going."

"But it will take your mind off Eben's bailing on you, and you won't be sitting here stewing all day, not like you have anything better to do 'til he gets back. . .". Melanie frowned. "Unless he's found someone else and he's not coming back, in which case this lunch only goes to two o'clock and you'd better. . .".

"First of all," Carrie interrupted, then paused to let herself find some breath, "Eben and I are not involved in any way. I don't own him and it doesn't interest me in the slightest whether he's found one somebody or fifty. Second, I am a professional with a job to do and I don't need Eben to fill my day. And third, if somebody doesn't come up something to do in ten seconds, everybody's fired."

"Well," offered Leon, stirring uncomfortably, "I'm waiting for a call back from Hendreik's office for a meeting this afternoon."

Carrie did her best to hide a wince and a long silence followed. She took a deep breath and turned to Melanie.

"Just where is this club?"

As they sped along the freeway in Melanie's silver Sebring convertible, Carrie lay back in her seat and silently moaned behind her dark sunglasses. She wished she could be anywhere but there. Or that she could shrink to a piece of dust and just blow away. Take your pick. Either one.

She glanced over at Melanie in her shimmering silver, high-cut dress and heels. She had said the meeting was casual, which accounted for Carrie's v-neck top, jeans and sandals which Melanie had insisted there was no time to change. The sandals were red, the jeans dark blue and the top very dark blue, almost black, in deference to her mood.

"Okay. Dish!", Melanie suddenly demanded.

"What?"

"Oh, come on! Eben? Your place? Three nights?"

"So?"

"All I know is that if it was me I'd have him surveyed and catalogued by now"

"Melanie! I thought you were seeing somebody."

"Carrie, give me some credit. I can prioritize."

Carrie sighed, then asked, "Is this a charitable club?", resuming her posture of resignation.

"Oh, absolutely. We never make any money."

"I don't have to make a speech, do I?"

"No, no. Honest. I swear."

"You didn't call anybody?" Three seconds of silence brought her glance sharply back in Melanie's direction. "Melanie?"

"Well, I did, but. . . ".

"Melanie!"

"I fixed it. At first I thought it was time you got over this press phobia of yours - it's been over a year since the, uh, thing, and I mean, 293 straight mentions on 'Entertainment Today' without ever once giving an interview? I mean, who gets that?"

"Melanie, how did you fix it?"

"Well, I called them and said you were cancelling and they wouldn't believe me, so I said your mother died, which I thought was alright because she's already, well, you know, but they wouldn't believe that, so. . .". She hesitated.

"How did you fix it?"

"I told them you were shacked up with a married actor in Beverly Hills and gave them an address. See? Fixed. Gee, I hope it's nobody you know."

Carrie was deprived of the opportunity to contemplate leaping from the car by its sudden veering off the freeway and slowing on the exit ramp. Within a few minutes they were pulling up to a stylish new building with a sign reading 'Bayshore Community Centre', having just passed through open gates with a smaller, incongruous sign warning, 'Private'.

"Just what is the name of this club?", she asked.

"Oh, we're the 'Burbank United Ladies League'."

"Burbank United. . .", Carrie muttered. "But Melanie, that spells. . .".

"We know what it spells," she replied defensively. "But nobody noticed until we were already registered."

"Why didn't you get it changed?"

"Because we already ordered ten thousand sheets of letterhead, and we couldn't send it back."

Melanie exited the car, followed reluctantly by Carrie, and they made their way through the manicured flower beds and up marble front steps to double glass front doors, framed in polished brass. If this was to be an execution, Carrie remarked to herself, at least it was to be an opulent one.

They continued through the doors, were met by a whoosh of extremely chilly air conditioning, and carried on down a broad hallway and more marble, until they reached a door labelled 'Meeting Room 5'. Melanie turned to face Carrie.

"Whatever you do, don't say anything to upset Margie."

"Who's Margie?"

"She's the President."

"And she's so easily upset?"

"Very."

"Then why did you elect her President?"

"We didn't elect her. She's just always been President." Melanie shrugged and lead the way through the door.

The room was fairly small and populated with about a dozen people who immediately fell silent. Then, as if on orders, they parted to reveal a tall, very thin, well-tanned woman in her fifties, with short metallic gold hair, wearing a white pant suit.

She strode towards them, extending a gold-laden hand to Melanie.

"Ah, Melanie. How are you?"

"Margie", Melanie responded, apparently not believing Margie sincerely wished to know how she was, "This is Carrie."

"Ah yes. You're a musician."

"Singer. . . actually", replied Carrie, taking the icy hand offered her, noting it hadn't been at all warmed by Melanie's. Or maybe it had. She shuddered.

"Of course. So good of you to come. I believe we've made room for you."

With that, the members obediently began to move, and Carrie for the first time noticed the odd layout of the room. The members were to be seated press conference style behind a long table with

Margie in the middle, before several long rows of seats which were apparently intended for no one.

As Melanie lead her away, Carrie inquired, "What did she mean by that?"

"Nothing. She likes you", she whispered, depositing Carrie beside Margie, and taking the next seat down for herself.

The dispersal of humanity revealed a table tucked into a corner upon which were a meagre-looking one-tray each of sandwiches and raw vegetables, with no dip, a pitcher of water and carafe of coffee. It didn't look overly appealing to Carrie, but she was starving and this was supposed to be a luncheon.

"When do we eat?", she asked.

"After. But don't even try it." Melanie indicated the table with a jerk of her head. "These people are like locusts. I always eat before I come."

Carrie's admonishment was cut off by a sharp rapping that turned out to be an actual gavel in the left hand of Margie.

"Everyone, it is time to come to order. I will note attendance for the Secretary. Margie is here. Also Stephanie, Laurie, Cathie, Hilary, Lindsay, Sally, Tracey, Lucy, Melanie and Gary."

Carrie's neck craned forward and she scanned the table until she spotted the previously unnoticed singular male presence.

"Mary is not here, and why is that?", she demanded, apparently expecting a vindication for the absent Mary.

"She's in her ninth month", someone replied.

"Oh yes. Very brave. Very commendable. Judy is not here, of course. That is as one might expect."

Carrie opened her mouth to ask but was met by Melanie's sideways glance and a subtle but firm shaking of her head.

"Everyone will now review last month's Minutes."

One of the surplus sheets of letterhead was passed along to Carrie which curiously contained nothing but the date of the previous meeting, attendance, and the time the meeting was apparently adjourned.

"What does Margie do for a living?", she asked of Melanie.

"Her husband owns the largest pre-owned luxury car dealership in the valley," she answered.

"With no changes or deletions to the Minutes", Margie continued, "A motion to pass the Minutes is carried. Any business arising out of the Minutes? Any new business?"

"Mary forwarded a topic for discussion", someone mentioned.

"Tremendous", replied Margie. "Excellent. But first, Melanie has brought a friend with her today. Carrie, stand so that everyone can see you."

Carrie did so to a smattering of light applause.

"This is the first time we've had Carrie. . .", Margie paused. "Hmmm. With Judy's absence, we may be seeing more of her. No promises of course, but time will tell."

Carrie sank back down with a feeling of being sucked into quicksand.

"Marvellous to have you", Margie went on. "So, my dear. On exactly what topic will you be speaking?"

CHAPTER 8

Carrie stood motionless in her silent courtyard where Melanie had left her a moment before, then sped away into the rushing traffic behind the slowly closing gate. Not much had been spoken between them on the drive back. She contemplated. Maybe her hastily improvised talk on the shifting economic base of the world music industry hadn't gone over. Maybe it was too short. Maybe it was too long.

In any event, the only questions it prompted were queries as to her opinion on various birth control methods, teenage abortion, breast implants and legalization of marijuana, obviously designed to ferret out whether she needed it, had it, wanted it or used it. This was followed by apparently obligatory hugs and kisses, enthusiastically thrust upon her and claimed in return by all, less so by Gary, and their departure without Carrie being able to determine in the slightest what actually had been accomplished by it all.

She moved to the front door, feeling that lately each entry to her house seemed to be on the crest of a thunderous wave of outside stress. She opened the door to welcome silence, although even the sound of her own singing would have been a relative relief. As she stepped inside, it was brought back to her that Eben probably wasn't there. It occurred to her that maybe he wasn't coming back, then labelled that juvenile to put it out of her mind.

Carrie sauntered to the living room to look at the sea, as was her custom. After a few seconds it gave her a start to notice Leon sitting at the table. The silence had belied his presence.

"Leon!"

"We're late," he replied. "We've got a meeting with Hendreik."

Carrie studied him. She had never before noticed Leon's striking resemblance to his namesake: the broad features, big brown eyes, soulful and sad, the golden mane of hair and dark beard - the latter two of course reversed in colour. A certain nobility.

"I'm not going."

"He's got a burr up his ass about something." Leon rose, as if to go. "You know him. I need you there. We'll need to do some fast maneuvering."

"I'm not going. You can handle it for me."

Leon paused, staring off to the side, his jaw clenched firm.

"You got something I need to know? I know you weren't serious this morning, but jeez, you might as well have been. I can't do this damned job in a vacuum. Do you want me out?"

Carrie was stunned.

"Leon, I. . .what's eating you?"

He picked up a newspaper lying face down on the table and slapped it down right side up. It was the latest issue of 'National Expulsor'. A large colour picture occupied two-thirds of the cover. It showed Carrie looking up into Eben's eyes with her hand grasping his arm. The remainder of the page held the caption: 'CARRIE TAKES HOME NEW PURCHASES'.

"I'll kill him."

"No you won't."

"Yes. I will."

"They wanted a restraining order last time. Do you know what that means? That means he tracks you down like usual and you don't even get the pleasure of telling him where to stick his camera - you have to run the other way. And if you don't, you're the one in trouble."

"It's a crock of shit."

"It's a pain in the ass and it's called 'Freedom of the Press'. It also goes with the territory. Someday you're gonna realize you don't get it both ways. But that isn't even the point, is it?"

Carrie threw him a questioning look.

"Why didn't you tell me about this?", he demanded, jabbing his finger at the picture.

"What's to tell? We went shopping. They took pictures. End of story."

"Do you even know the slightest thing about this guy?"

"I know lots about him. He comes from Canada. He was an architect, up to five years ago."

"So, what. You're a big item now? Don't you think that's something I should know?"

"We are not an item. We're just. . .close."

"You're close", he repeated.

"Yes", she concluded, feeling slightly triumphant.

Leon paused. "So you would know where he spent his time today."

Carrie felt her lower lip compressing into her upper. She spoke with exaggerated control.

"You are not my father. Nothing has happened that I can't handle. Go look in on the instrumentals, Leon. It's not your concern. It's not anybody's concern."

Leon stared at her and as he did so his anger seemed to dissipate before her eyes into a look she could only describe as mournfulness.

"That's where you're wrong. Absolutely," he replied, and moved towards the kitchen door. Halfway through he paused, then turned back.

"Be careful," he said, then disappeared.

Carrie waited, arms down straight at her sides, fists clenched, barely able to suppress herself. When she heard the front door close she let out an "Ohhhhh!", of exasperation. She knew she had to do something - anything. She started off in several different directions until she settled on a drink. Off to the kitchen, and a tumbler full of ice cubes and some sort of fruit mix later, she was headed for the deck and a lounge chair, topping off with rum on the way. She took several big gulps of the concoction beneath the warms rays of the sun, but didn't really notice either.

"Leon", she muttered with not so mild disdain. Underneath it all she knew he meant well. He was doing his job. He cared about her. But her attempts at these thoughts were constantly overridden by "Damn him"s.

"Damn that Eben. Where is he?", she exclaimed and looked around as if she might have overlooked him before. He had ruined their perfect afternoon together by disappearing without a trace, and leaving her with the horror of a day that was apparently her life. No, that was too extreme. It was simply a bad day. To say otherwise meant that what Leon had intimated was right, and she was hung up on Eben. That couldn't be right. They hadn't even kissed. And if Eben felt that way, surely he would've felt obliged to advise her of his whereabouts. So he wasn't and she wasn't. So why was she so angry with him and seemingly so desperate for him to return?

The thoughts revolved in her mind over and over and over. Each time she would make a brilliant and exhaustive argument for one side, then repeat the process for the other just as effectively, for she was fully capable of such a thing, to no apparent conclusion. Only the click of the front door finally interjected, and she was confronted with two immediate realities: that the sun had already set, and that she really had to pee.

Nevertheless, she rushed to the door, feigning nonchalance only at the last possible second.

The anger she had lived in for hours seemed to have vanished to be replaced by relief: relief that he was back and safe, and in an indefinable way, so was she. She felt a tear rising, which she chose to ascribe to hurt feelings, and suppress.

"Oh. Eben. You're back."

"Yes. Hi", he replied. "Sorry I've been so long."

"Has it been long? I'm not sure. I didn't know when you left."

"Yes, I'm sorry about that, but I didn't want to wake you."

"Oh, no mind. Of course, it did cross my mind you might have gone back on your journey. You know, 'There's always a time to move on'."

"But then you saw my knapsack wasn't gone."

Carrie paused. "Right", she replied. "I saw your knapsack."

Eben smiled. "I got you something. I hope you don't mind."

"But, how. . .?"

He paused at the door. "I've been at Peter's working all day. He advanced me the rest. Of course, I owe a few more days."

Her head tilted slightly, and a little smile came to her that she had forgotten existed. "You really didn't need to". The smile turned mischievous, and she craned her neck in the direction of the door. "Any hints?"

"Well, it's small and gold."

"Oh Eben, you really shouldn't. . .".

She was interrupted by his opening of the door, and the sight of a small, bronze-coloured mass of curls, encompassing what appeared to be a dog. Somewhere in the curls she spied two black eyes and a nose, and a little pink tongue.

"Well?", he inquired, making her realize he might wish for more than her two raised eyebrows and open mouth.

"It's. . .adorable," she managed to reply, and with a slight shaking of her head, "But. . .why?"

"It occurred to me that someday you'll be tired of me and I'll be gone," he grinned, "and you'll need someone." He bent over, scooped up the dog and placed it in Carrie's arms.

"She's from a broken home." He gently covered the dog's ears and whispered, "Apparently he wanted her, so she wanted her, so he wouldn't have her, so she refused to take her." He smiled and removed his hands. "She's housebroken, has her shots, answers to her name, and comes with a 30 day money back guarantee. Kind of like me." He laughed.

She laughed too. "But I assume you're not fixed." He returned her smile. "What's her name?"

"Sadie", he replied.

Carrie looked into the curly face, then frowned. "Hmmm", she paused, thinking. "Whatever we do, don't let Melanie take her to her club."

Exotic, international cuisine at a little oceanfront place she knew was suggested by Carrie to celebrate Eben's new, albeit temporary, job. She got ready faster than she'd thought possible, and within twenty minutes they were strolling southward along the beach. Eben wore slacks, shirt and leather jacket, all selected for him the day before. He kept to the land side to protect his shoes and to keep Sadie out of the water, who he led on a hastily improvised collar and leash.

Carrie wore a halter top of blue-green, and now and again the balmy breeze playfully tossed her hair about her bare, tanned shoulders. This revealed gold hoop earrings, which reflected lights from the houses they passed by, only to disappear again behind her dark curtain of hair, cascading back to its place. Her skirt of a swirl of green and blue and beige was calf-length, but she still kept carefully to the sand between the waves and the path taken by Eben. Her sandals hung from two fingers of her right hand, and were flung about carelessly as she gesticulated, describing her day and commenting on the day described in return by Eben. Her left hand she had quietly snuck into Eben's on the pretence of balancing herself to remove her shoes, and there it had un-apologetically remained, seemingly without opposition from him.

Their path was lit by the moon out over the water, not quite full but shining with an extreme brightness, dimmed only slightly by the many accompanying stars. Even the satellites and jets overhead could do nothing to compete. A question was forming in Carrie's mind as to why the sun had recently been so comparatively dull, when Eben spoke.

"I still can't believe you let Melanie suck you in."

"Oh, I'll get over it", she replied. "You know, some therapy, a partial lobotomy...." She smiled.

"You've got to wonder what motivates a person to join something like that. She must be trying to make up for a lack of something."

"Oh, she just wants to make a difference. We all do. She just hasn't found the right place."

"You realize she's envious of you."

"Well, I suppose. I've had more success."

"Hmmm", replied Eben, sounding unconvinced. Then, after a pause, "Do you suppose it comes with the profession?"

"What?"

"Dissatisfaction with oneself."

"I don't know", she answered. "Not that I've experienced firsthand."

The houses to their left were now side by side by side, and the low-lying string of lights ahead had grown to reveal a pier, which extended the lights from the line of the houses out over the water. They climbed a set of stairs near the base of the pier and found, much to Carrie's irritation, that there was an entrance fee of $2.00, which had previously been free. This led to lighthearted cracks, such as, "Don't sit anywhere - they'll come charge us", and "It costs $12.50 to look at the water", only slightly tinged with sarcasm. They wound their way through a maze of little shacks advertising the sale of bait, souvenirs and french fries, until Carrie found what she wanted. From the one labelled only as "Mike's", she ordered two falafel and coke combos with some scraps and water for Sadie, to which Eben feigned surprise that she wasn't ordering in Arabic. They found a bench against the south side of the pier, darkened except for a few scattered muted yellow lights which reflected off of the water below, and with few people about.   Eben pronounced the falafels, "Anything but awful", and when they were done they sat sideways on the bench facing each other, silent until she noticed him gazing fixedly over his shoulder at something in the distance. She waited a while to see how long he would continue, then through a teasing smile said, "You know, much more of this and I'll start to have an abandonment complex."

"Oh, I'm sorry," he replied. "It's just...is that an amusement park down there?"

"Yes," she answered, and glanced the few miles down the beach to where the dark outline of a ferris wheel and roller coaster and a few other rides sat silent in the moonlight. "It's been there forever. I think it's still open on the weekends, but it's one of those places I can't go anymore." She gave him a sheepish smile, and her eyes returned to the park. Slowly it began to come to life to her: bright garish lights lit up, the wheel began to turn, the rides to spin, and small bug-like cars to traverse the tracks of the coaster. She heard the far-off laughter and ecstatic screams mingled with the blaring music. Then she was in among them, huddling together as the coaster car went over the top, necking at the top of the ferris wheel, splitting a hotdog because that's all the money they had.

"It reminds me of one not too far from where I grew up," Eben continued. "Same great old rickety park. Roller coaster, fun house, little train ride. Then they tore it down for condos and put up a plaque saying how great it had all been."

She had been pulled from her memory, and as she turned back she knew what she'd see - a dark silhouette like the burnt-out remains of someone's dreams. It wasn't his fault, and was probably for the best. But still, she felt like she wasn't quite ready to detach herself from that feeling.

"I used to go there, sometimes", she began hesitantly, "a long time ago, when I first moved here. I was living with this guy. He was a songwriter. We didn't have much of anything. I could say we were living on our dreams, but that would be corny."

"Living on love?" he offered.

"No, it wasn't like that. I mean, we...you know. But what I loved was him - the person. It was like we were perfectly complementary, you know?"

Eben gave a slight smile and nod. She looked down the beach again.

"But it was hard for him. I could sing in clubs - that's where Leon found me. But if his songs didn't sell he had nothing, no matter how good they were. That was the hard part. He was so idealistic about what he wrote, but he needed success to survive. Then one day he...." She lifted a hand to wipe away a tear, then shook her head. "It was just before I found my success. He left me his songs in his note."

Carrie turned to look Eben in the eye.

"Don't you see?" she asked. "My albums were all his songs."

They looked away simultaneously, he downward in a frown and she out over the water. "I used all of them," she continued, her voice breaking. After a moment he looked back.

"But by now", he queried, "don't you believe you've proven him wrong?"

Carrie turned to him and seriously considered. "Yes," she replied. "I suppose I do."

They began their walk back up the beach in contemplative silence. The air was cool and still, which made the crash of the waves as they came, white and tumbling out of the darkness, almost jarring. She slipped her hand into his again, feeling it to be territory fairly won and therefore unrelinquishable. But his hand was warm compared to all of her, and the difference caused her to shiver slightly. In an instant his jacket was over her shoulders, and she was enveloped in his warmth and the smell of his cologne. She looked at him and smiled.

"I'm sorry about before", she offered.

"No. Sometimes I get too intrusive. I don't know. Like there's a second me or something." He paused and looked at the breakers, and neither pursued it. "Those waves just seem to appear out of nowhere", he remarked absently.

"Yes, but thankfully we're off the pier." It was met by a quizzical look. "This would be costing me a fortune!"

They laughed together, his arm moved around her shoulder, and she was drawn in close. They continued like this, but in silence. She could feel his body next to her, supporting her, indulgently keeping her upright while she gazed up at the stars, wishing it wouldn't end.

They entered the house on tiptoes and in whispers for no reason other than that it was silent and the hour late. They made a bed for Sadie in the utility room, then Carrie led Eben tentatively down the hall to just outside the bedrooms, where she turned to face him.

"I had a wonderful time."

"So did I," he replied. "Thank you. For dinner."

"Oh, you're welcome. So exotic and yet so chic", and they laughed.

She looked into the eyes of the man who had befriended her, who obviously cared about her, and who she cared about in return. She felt passion rise within her and supposed he felt the same. But there was something else she couldn't define or explain: some invisible thread of unrealized thought - minute but powerful - that held her back. She decided to quickly kiss him goodnight and did so. Uttering a soft, "Sweet dreams, Eben", she stole through her bedroom door and gently closed it behind her. But inexplicably, the kiss left behind had lingered far longer than she had planned.

CHAPTER 9

Rather than analysing the kiss, which would have been usual for her, Carrie fell right to sleep, enveloped in the pure intoxication of it all. The next morning she was enjoying a dream in which the kiss was being played out continuously: enjoying, at least, until it became obvious that the dream was stubbornly refusing to move any further. Then, just as some progress seemed to be made, she was sharply awakened by the sound of male voices in heated debate. For a while she lay there listening, but not listening, unable to will herself to move, thinking. Maybe they'll just kill each other and let me go back to sleep.

"Oooh, somebody's going to pay for this one," she declared, and threw the covers aside. She took time to get dressed - panties weren't necessarily recommended for refereeing - then stepped out into the hallway. She quickened her pace when the voices became combative.

On the landing she came upon Eben and Leon, faces flushed,

and Melanie in the background, with an expression of moderate zeal, perhaps taking notes.

"What in the world is going on?" Carrie demanded.

"Why don't you tell her," snapped Leon to Eben.

"Apparently I'm being interrogated."

"Yeah?", Leon retorted. "Well, I ain't gettin' too many answers."

"Leon. How could you?"

"How could I what? Protect my client from some lying scum who isn't who he claims to be?"

Carrie stood transfixed, looking at Leon. The question, "What?", formed itself on her mouth, but no sound came out.

"Go ahead and ask him," Leon went on. His name ain't even Christopher at all. It's Janus. Eben Janus. Probably uses his real first name 'cause he's afraid of slipping up."

Carrie turned to Eben who was staring downward, hands in pockets. Presently he looked up and into her eyes.

"Is it true?", she whispered, feeling tears welling in her eyes.

He paused then answered a quiet "Yes." He moved a step towards her and she felt herself move a quarter step back. At that moment, she hated Leon.

"Carrie", he continued, "I told you when I left home it was because things didn't feel right." He glanced with a look of irritation at the other two. "That included my name. Christopher is my middle name, so I just carried on using that."

She looked into his eyes whose depth she seemed unable to penetrate. But his gaze never faltered from hers, and she turned with a plaintive look to Leon.

"Ask yourself, Carrie," he challenged. "What else has he lied about?"

She looked back and forth between them while waiting for an answer she couldn't find. Her lips parted slightly in the futile hope that something would come out to quell the agonizing silence, when the front door opened. All four heads turned to see a man: expensive suit, expensive shoes, expensive haircut, who shot Carrie a look of distain, then Eben a look of loathing. His eyes moved momentarily to Leon, who betrayed nothing, but who frowned and seemed to look slightly downward. The man's gaze shifted back to Carrie and he strode stridently to just before her, pinning her with his glare.

She felt very small and very alone, in an ocean of confusion and uncertainty. However, her primary thoughts were of something else. For sure he had been away for a month, around the world on business. The two of them had rarely spoken, and made no attempt to meet. But she was now overcome with the incredible realization that, for the last five days at least, she had not even once remembered he existed.

The man's expression heightened to one of seething contempt. He glanced again at Eben, which seemed to infuriate him more. Then it happened in an instant: his sharp turn back to Carrie, his curse, "You miserable slut!", the lifting of his arm to strike and Eben's grasping of his hand, pulling it back and causing the man to sink to the floor with an agonized cry. He lay there for an brief moment, then struggled to his feet, rubbing his apparently useless wrist and breathing awkwardly. His anger was not gone but he could no longer manifest it, so he stumbled to the door and out, issuing a final, ineffectual, "Slut!", before he disappeared.

For a while no one stirred. Then Eben quietly moved down the hall, seeming to look through rather than at anyone. Melanie was next: appearing somewhat in shock, she silently crept to the far end of the livingroom. Carrie and Leon stood mute and separated by the width of the landing. She with arms crossed, one leg straight out and resting on its heel, lips pursed in a frown, glaring at him. He with left hand in pocket, right hand rubbing his beard, slightly swaying, looking sideways at the floor. Finally Leon stated, "I think I'd better...", and pointing his way to the door, went through it. Carrie followed Eben's path down the hall.

She found him in the guestroom, looking somewhat lost. She started to say something several times, then finally asked, "Where did you learn to do that?"

"When I was in Korea, I got a job...."

"Never...never mind," she interjected, waving him off, then put her hand to her forehead. She couldn't think of where to start.

'I think I should be going."

"No, Eben, don't. Please. Just...". She heard the front door open and close. "Just give me a minute", she pleaded, and hurried back down the hall.

Leon was standing there, and after a moment's pause stated matter-of-factly, "Well, he's not going to sue. Too much publicity, I guess." He paused again. "I suppose it wouldn't look too good for the Lion of Wall Street to have his ass kicked by some...." He caught her reproachful look. 'Well, anyway, I have a ten o'clock with Hendriek, and he says if somebody doesn't show he's going ahead without us."

She studied him for a moment. Then her face softened to one of reflection.

"Give me a few minutes. I'll go with you", she said quietly, and turned to go back down the hall.

Eben now sat on the very edge of the guest bed, and as she entered he softly spoke.

"You don't owe me an explanation. And I'm not stupid. You're constantly at risk, I know that, but there's nothing I can do to set your mind at ease. So you will always be wondering. Unless I go."

Carrie took a moment to consider what he had said. "Eben", she began, "I have to go downtown. I can't get out of it. Please just stay here until I get back and we can talk." At that moment she felt strangely detached from the subject of her and Eben, but one reality couldn't be shaken - that if he left she could never find him again. "Please."

After a brief moment he gave a slight nod. She went to him, bent down, and with her hands lightly on his shoulder, kissed him gently on the cheek, then left.

The high-rise building which housed the Company was distinct in its indistinctiveness. Its outer shell was composed completely of mirrored glass so that, by reflecting everything around it, it gave the appearance of being everything else but itself.

They had arrived in Leon's ten year old Buick. It was the same car he had when Carrie met him, and she often badgered him as to why he didn't get something nicer. His response was that before he couldn't afford anything, and now that he could afford it, who did he need to impress? On the positive side it allowed them to travel somewhat under the radar.

The ride in the mirrored elevator from the parking garage to the top floor gave Carrie time to reflect on the trip in. Both had kept to a business-like silence which was just as well - there was no time to debate what had happened that morning, and no need to discuss what was going to occur at the meeting, as they had no idea what it was about.

The elevator opened to the familiar lobby, opulently cold, also mirrored. As they sat waiting - Carrie had recently given up pushing past the reception desk when Hendreik had a security lock put on his door - she pondered the meaning of mirrors. They make space look bigger than it is, multiply light which is artificial also, and give an endless reflective image of what really isn't there. Who cleans this stuff?, she wondered.

They were summoned to Hendreik's office, which was a decorative extension of the lobby: leather and metallic furniture, mirrors on three sides, and spectacular ocean view on the fourth. Hendreik sat behind his desk with his back to the vista, feet up, in the last throes of a telephone conversation, as though his time was too valuable to waste thirty seconds idly waiting for them to arrive from the lobby. Half-turned away, he motioned for them to sit. Leon did so, but Carrie remained standing, studying him: medium height; thin; longish, straight hair, either black streaked grey or the reverse; handlebar mustache dyed black. Caps. Black and white collarless striped shirt and black pants. Manicured polished toenails in leather sandals. She recalled he had an accent she'd never been able to place, then started to wonder whether anything about the man, or indeed, the office, was real. She began to doubt the view, and was mentally retracing their steps to see if she really was facing west, when the call was completed. She seized the initiative.

"The cover is completely unacceptable," she declared. "I don't give a damn about your computer. It's not me and I won't have it on my album".

Hendreik stayed seated. "Suggestions are fine", he began, "and this will be treated as one. Perhaps something can be done to your satisfaction. But as Mr. Speckman will inform you, final decision on virtually all matters - album design, song selection, hiring of musicians - rests with the Company. We are here today to consult. So...." Once again he waved for her to sit.

Carrie glanced at Leon, who seemed intent only on trying to decipher what this was all about, so she acquiesced. She had never seen Hendreik so apparently empowered. The listing of the company's contractual rights was in and of itself, foreboding.

Hendreik sat with one leg crossed over the other, elbows on the chair arms, fingertips pressed together to form a sort of inverted V, and went on.

"The Company has been moving forward in a new direction - a trendier sort of sound. We've hired new artists, have a number of new projects coming out and, well...no matter. The short of it is, we don't want any of our current projects to be left, how shall we say, in the dust? We would like you to record a few more...", he paused, "...edgier possibilities for inclusion in the album. These have been written by some of our most talented young writers. Then we'll see. The Company's new image cannot be undercut by the old. Sentimentality is the death-knell of the music industry." He paused again, and swivelled to glance out the window. "Studio time has been booked starting tomorrow."

Carrie and Leon sat stunned. Hendreik seemed in no hurry for a reply, miking the silence. Finally Leon articulated the obvious.

"The tour starts in less than two weeks. Even if there's no change in the album, there's no time."

"The first weeks of the tour have already been shifted to the end", Hendreik cooly replied, turning back. "The necessary arrangements have been made."

"The band", Carrie demanded. "They have no experience playing what you've got in mind. It would take them weeks just to practice, much less have time to record."

"The tracks for the new songs have already been laid down by our own studio artists", he replied with a barely concealed smugness. "Except for yours and Miss Black's. If the band can come up to speed in the next few weeks, then they might be included in the tour...subject to consultation with the Company, of course. He smiled and rose, signalling an end to the meeting. "But don't worry. These are mere experiments which may not amount to anything. One wouldn't even call them requirements. Let us call them...kind requests."

For Carrie and Leon the return trip was, if possible, even quieter that the one downtown. But it gave her time for cold reflection. How could they have let this happen - that Hendreik and his plans had gotten so far past them. After a long while it was Leon who spoke.

"Maybe it will all come to nothing", he suggested. But Carrie wasn't reassured.

"There's one thing I just don't get", she declared. "This album will make money. They've all made money. Why change anything now?"

There was a pause, and she heard Leon quietly sigh.

"I got a theory about that", he replied, "but I don't think you'd believe me."

She turned to face him and braced herself for what was to come.

"The albums each made a lot of money," he continued. "Each one made more than the last." He looked over in her direction. "But the rate of increase, decreased. So the last one barely made more than the one before."

"You mean to them, I'm on my way out?" She was incredulous.

"To those bastards, yes."

"And this tune-up is my salvation."

"I think it may be even more warped than that", he answered. Maybe they're looking for an excuse. Maybe they want you to fail."

CHAPTER 10

"That's it", said a voice, seemingly disembodied.

"Thanks guys", Carrie replied, and reached up to remove the headphones cupped over her ears. She began to stretch her neck in all possible directions to try to remove the kinks. Twelve days, twelve songs. Same number as on the album, she noted, then glossed over the coincidence. The album took much longer to record. Not her natural stuff, she thought, but not bad, not too bad at all. That bastard Hendreik. Failure my ass.

She hopped down from her elevated chair and headed through the door, grabbing a fresh bottle of water and issuing a final wave to the boys behind the glass. As she headed down the hall she paused at the window to another sound studio, where Melanie had been reposited for eleven days, recording backup harmonies for each of Carrie's efforts from the previous day. She listened intently for a moment, noting the strong, assertive voice she already knew

Melanie possessed, but realizing also that it was probably much better suited to this type of music than her own. Just then Melanie looked up and gave her a big smile, and a wink. Carrie mildly returned the smile, then turned away down the hall. She wondered as an afterthought what Melanie had been doing with all her spare time, since her recording schedule was about half that of Carrie's. This prompted her to spend the drive home reviewing the previous two weeks since it had all begun.

She hadn't wondered why she hadn't wondered about the seeming lack of any residual feelings for her now ex-boyfriend. She laughed wryly as it suddenly occurred to her she may have lost two boyfriends at one stroke. Was the first really such a total write-off? Their relationship to her was like a defunct piece of office equipment: capable of apparently wonderful things when new that, when viewed now, upon reflection, seemed tired and obsolete. Certainly she knew they had had some enjoyable and memorable times together. However, for whatever reason, she was just unable to recall any, or recall him at all except when she deliberately forced herself. And since that unavoidably meant wasting time that could be spent happily daydreaming about Eben, it was not going to happen. Work was a priority - exes were not.

With Eben it was so different. She didn't just look forward to seeing him, she yearned for it. But it wasn't like her former love, whose gift of song-writing she had so idolized. Eben touched her in an indefinable way. Was it simply that she had vaulted into the security of another relationship on the rebound? This she doubted. For one thing, there was nothing secure about it. And besides, it was more like on the pre-bound. But she had barely seen Eben, with her recording by day, often going late, and him working a lot of nights at the Cantina. She had detected a certain distance between them. It was like trying to cultivate a romantic relationship while walking on broken glass. It was a situation she reflected upon almost constantly, trying to determine its origin. Each time she came to the same conclusion: the onset of their semi-professional relationship. But she would began the process of analysing again, as now, as one recounts a bittersweet heartbreak to oneself, over and over, not expecting any different result, as if in a state of narcotic attraction. She thought back to the day of the meeting with Hendreik, when she returned to the house.

Carrie had found Eben in the living room, on the far end of the sofa, staring out at the sea. She had resisted the temptation to peek into the guest room to see if his knapsack, and therefore he, were ready to go, and deciding to go at it blind, crept in and eased herself down at the sofa's opposite end. She hadn't had much time or energy to think things between her and Eben through since leaving Hendreik's office, but she knew she didn't want it to end.

Eben straightened where he sat and gave her a slight smile. "How'd the meeting go?", he offered.

Carrie smiled back then looked down at her feet, now bare, although she hadn't relinquished her navy blue suit jacket and skirt. "Okay, I guess", she answered. She brought her knees up and wrapped her arms around them, feeling very small. She rested the side of her head on her knees and looked at him. "Eben", she went on, "before this morning I wasn't sure what we might have together - now I'm even less sure. But I don't want you to leave before we... before we figure it all out."

Eben returned to gazing at the ocean, but presently replied, without turning, "I'm not built to just go on living here, waiting."

"I know that. I've been thinking about that. The truth is...the truth is the meeting didn't go like we thought. I'm kind of heading into unchartered waters - for me anyway. I really need someone to confide in, officially, like an advisor."

He turned and his eyes met hers. "I don't know anything about the music industry."

"And that's what I need right now. I'm too close to it. Leon's too close. I need you to just tell me what you think. On call at all times.

And you can still keep working at the Cantina if you want. What do you think? For room and board."

Eben had reflected for a while and either couldn't, or wouldn't, find anything in the idea to object to. He asked when she wanted him to start. With her reply of "immediately", she began to recount the details of the meeting. He sat listening intently, then when she finished, reminded her that he was to work at one o'clock. He got up to leave but at the landing turned back to face her.

"I do have one immediate bit of advice for you".

"Really", she replied, slightly surprised. "What is it"?

"Stop regretting."

Her eyebrows raised as she looked at him. But in a moment a slight smile of recognition came to her.

Eben returned the smile, waved his hand and was gone.

This time, as she pulled into her courtyard and garage, Carrie had no expectation of finding Eben at home. He would be working, she noted to herself, which gave her a sudden inspiration. Maybe she could catch up with him for dinner, which led to a further idea. Maybe she could squeeze in a run.

She sprinted in from the garage to the house; exchanged salutations with Bella and received an updated doggie report; accepted Sadie's energetic greetings intermixed with vocal condemnations at her having been gone so long; quickly accompanied her in and out of the green-space that had been established for her in the courtyard; then hurried toward her bedroom. As it was, she noted the phenomenon in her life that, once she discovered she had a few extra hours, she promptly set to overfilling them and, as a result, immediately became in a hurry. The shower of abandoned clothes barely had time to settle before ice blue shorts and a tank top were donned and the deck was gained. Once apologies and promises of a later walk were made through the glass door, she was southward on her run, stopwatch left ticking behind.

As her body, deprived of its usual warmup due to time constraints, began to grind and clank its way to something approaching an acceptable rhythm, Carrie began to wonder how long it had been since her last run, then realized with chagrin that, discounting the aborted jog with Eben, she hadn't run since his arrival. This thing with Hendreik had temporarily knocked her off her schedule and her stride. But as she warmed, she perceived that the deviation seemed to have been of some benefit. She felt more rested - stronger too. Hendreik's power trip had been a pain, but was done and now an irritation at most. She wasn't above experimenting once in a while, or lending a hand to some up-and-coming songwriters. If a couple of edgy songs meant she gave a boost to the company, yet again, so what? Maybe a slight crossover would bring in more listeners to her kind of music. She felt at ease with that thought, and let her forearms drop to her sides, shaking them loosely to relax herself, then returning them to horizontal.

By the time she had made her turn around and come halfway back, she was in a rhythm and felt no ill-effect from the lay-off. What came now was hunger: sudden, ill-timed, seemingly unconnected and out of place, it began to consume her. I'm so hungry I could eat my hand, she joked to herself. For distraction she began to recite the Cantina Limbo's menu from memory, but this had the predictable, opposite effect. At least, when I get there, she reasoned, I'll know what I want.

Beyond this, the whole ordeal was making her run what she was sure was a personal best. This, however, was never to be substantiated. A hundred yards from her finish line she veered toward the base of the cliff below the Cantina, not slowing her pace in the least. As she arrived at the door, she briefly rationalized the early dinner on the grounds that it meant more time with Eben, and began to review her meal selection: cold shrimp, arrived at based on its brevity of preparation and certainty of availability. She opened the door, but stopped of a sudden, overcome by a brand new problem. I must look a wreck, she thought, then declared out loud, "Oh well. I have to eat them. They don't have to eat me", and skipped through the door.

Carrie launched herself onto the deck of the Cantina and in the direction of the stairs, but was met halfway there by the sight of Eben racing towards her, having obviously responded to her frantic pushing of the electronic buzzer, and having also, at least temporarily, gotten over his distrust of the rickety stairs. She wasn't prepared, having been thinking only of her impending starvation and not that she hadn't seen him for what seemed like forever. As they came together, she forgot herself and almost jumped into his arms. But she may have pressed the buzzer a little too frantically. Peter too, appeared at the top of the stairs, looking concerned. She called out to him over Eben's shoulder.

"Paedro! Traigame veinte camarones con una botella de agua, por favor! Rapido! Es una emergencia!"

As Peter hustled away she returned her gaze to Eben, with a smile. "Table and champagne for two, please. Something with a view, I think."

"Are you expecting someone?", he replied with a grin.

"I don't know. What time do you get off?"

"Hmmm. I think the boss might just let me off early. I'll go see."

As she watched him go she nodded with a contented smile and quietly murmured, "Bueno."

Eben returned to the usual table and his usual seat, and gave Carrie a happy nod.   "Are we celebrating?", he asked.

"Most definitely."

"What?"

"The hopeful end to this Hendreik nonsense."

"He backed off?"

"No, not yet. But I realized a couple of songs isn't the end of the world. If you can't change someone, you have to change your attitude towards him, right? I'm at peace with it." She gave a resigned smile and nodded.

He looked at her for a moment under raised eyebrows. "So you won't be needing my services any longer?"

"I'd like to keep you on an ongoing retainer. Let's face

it - Hendreik's still in the picture. Who knows what else might come up."

Eben smiled, and went off to get the champagne.

A scant hour later, dinner was done, clothes were changed, and Sadie retrieved. The three were walking southward along the beach and Carrie was feeling mellow, and had a slight buzz from the champagne. A vigorous but balmy breeze had picked up, necessitating the selection of a high ponytail on her part, as well as jeans and a greyish-blue sweatshirt, but little other inconvenience. The wind cut off the top of the breakers as they rolled in one by one, blowing away the frothy mist and leaving them razor-sharp. The sun was dropping to the horizon in a sky far more clear than of late, over a uniformly indigo sea. For Carrie, the tour was straight ahead, Eben and Sadie were by her side, and the hope was that the re-institution of hand-holding with Eben wasn't far away.

As Carrie's bare feet swept across the cool, fine sand, she glanced up and down the coast. She found no one, the beach-goers seemingly having retired at their leisure to dinner, not sharing in her premature pangs of hunger. She looked up the beach again, then started to glance out over the water, but her attention was drawn back. Something was out of place, although nothing in particular could be discerned. Then it struck her - it wasn't so much an object as a movement. At that instant, Sadie began to bark wildly, and to frantically pull Eben forward. Hurrying to keep up, Carrie soon spotted the source of the excitement. Some small, white animal was moving about in a jerky motion, ahead on the sand. As they came closer it took the form of a seagull, but it seemed strangely frozen in a grotesque, unnatural pose. Suddenly frightened by the barking, it started up and, flapping its wings spastically, scuttled a few yards farther away. Carrie motioned for Eben to stay back with the dog, then cautiously moved forward. The seagull looked at her, but naturally enough, almost indifferently. Then, with a shock, she realized the problem. A virtually invisible fishing line was wound around it, making it unable to extend its wings properly, unable to lower one leg completely, and probably unable to eat.

She felt her heart begin to sink and, inexplicably to her, tears began to brim up in her eyes. But she quickly pushed that aside and began to formulate a course of action. She went to Eben, instructing him to take Sadie back and return as soon as possible with a blanket, cardboard box and scissors. She then began to review all probable actions of the seagull and possible reactions by her designed to keep it contained. She concluded she was prepared for anything except it escaping over the ocean, which didn't seem likely in its present state. As in business affairs, Carrie kept emotion to a minimum, and yet she was aware of a certain desperation in her thoughts. Certainly the seagull faced the possibility of starvation and maybe even threats from predators if she couldn't free it. But there seemed to be even more at stake that was beyond her to define.

Now, she thought, if it will only sit still and relax until the cavalry comes. Apparently, it had other ideas. In that particular trait of animals to not recognize those who have their best interests at heart, and what is best for them, the bird began to stumble away. It was like stranded Pilot whales which, after the herculean efforts of humans to push them out sea, return to shore once again. Carrie chose a roundabout path by the cliff in order to cut off the escape and coax it back toward home. However, it appeared to immediately sense the end-around and, panic-stricken, began to take flight in the opposite direction. She found it amazing to see the reserve of energy it still possessed. It flew haphazardly and just a few feet above the ground, but fast enough that Carrie, at full stride, could barely keep up. Still, she stuck to her strategy, carefully scrutinizing the terrain ahead to plan the most advantageous route. But every so often she would be surprised as she sank to her ankles in a soft patch of sand that she had thought to be quite firm, or was sideswiped by a rogue wave that, out of nowhere, soaked her to her knees. Each time she lost ground and yet she persevered, with no sense of futility, confident in herself, unable to accept the realization that she couldn't overtake the seagull, much less force it back. It was like trying to overtake the past - no matter how hard you try, it just keeps inching away. Only after a half mile, comprehending that she was likely robbing of it of what little energy it still had, threatening its very existence, did she let go and stop. She knelt to the sand, watching the seagull dwindle away to nothingness in the distance.

Carrie stared on, vainly waiting for the bird to come back to her, full of emptiness and oblivious of the now darkened sky. Finally she raised herself up for what felt like the last time, and began to meander numbly homeward. Her thoughts were not focussed - there was disappointment and helplessness, but more than that: a vague self-knowledge of an almost ineffectual state. She wandered on until she began obliquely aware of Eben, hurrying towards her along the beach. He slowed when he saw her, and after a few second's study of her face, stopped completely and let her drift into his arms. The embrace, though not insincere, was somewhat perfunctory, but she barely took notice. He turned with her, to put an arm behind her, as a support to guide her the rest of the way. They reached her darkened house and continued up the stairs, where they had started off only an hour before.

As they entered the living room, Carrie vaguely noted the urgent flash of the answering machine on the desk beside the door. Almost disinterestedly she went to it, as one works through mundane household chores by rote, and pushed the message retrieval button. It spoke.

"Carrie? This is Leon. Look, we've got to talk. I heard from Hendreik. He wants all twelve - the whole damned album. And, I'm sorry, there's more. Zack and the band are out."

CHAPTER 11

Carrie knew just what to do. She had known for a long time - had been preparing for a long time, reviewing her options, planning and re-planning her strategies. Sooner or later, this was going to happen. Hendreik was that type of person everyone faces in their work: essential and superfluous; arrogant and unsure; abusive and needy; alternately requiring a velvet glove and an iron fist. He had always been a thorn in the side of her career, but something had changed, he had become inexplicably empowered. It was going to stop. Now.

She flipped through a business card index on the desk then, finding the one she was looking for, picked up the receiver and began to dial. As she waited for an answer she noticed Eben standing by the door, patient and forgotten. With an, "Oh!", of recognition, she made motion to him of drinking from a wine glass and two fingers, then brushed him in the direction of the kitchen with her hand. The call connected.

"Carrie Ralston for Mr. Williamson, please", she requested, and began to picture the man she was waiting for: medium height but large and imposing, despite twinkling blue eyes and an amiable smile set in his full, reddish face, all used for effect when required she was sure. Well dressed, always, with the exception of an ever-present blue shirt with white collar. A huge gold wristwatch enveloped one of the massive wrists and several chunky gold and diamond rings wound 'round the thick fingers. For some reason she knew he must be a golfer.

"Mr. Williamson. I'm sorry to bother you at home so.... Okay. I'm sorry. Bill.... Yes, it has been a while.... Yes, you're right, it was. We had a great time visiting. Do you still have.... Oh. No kidding. Bora Bora. And how are Bebe and the kids? Really. You must be very proud. Listen, I don't want to trouble you too much, but something's come up that I think needs your attention. Hendreik has made some...artistic decisions on the new album that need review. I don't think they're going to fly. Uh-huh. I knew you'd understand. Well that's very nice of you to say. The company's vital to me too. No, I think it can wait until the morning, but he has put us a bit behind. Thank you, Bill, I really appreciate it. Yes, we'll have to do that soon. Take care."

Carrie laid down the receiver and let out a quiet sigh, then noticed Eben on the sofa with two glasses of wine, as per instructions, waiting for her. She raced to him, scooped up one glass and flung herself on the cushions, back against the arm, feet on his lap. She flourished her wineglass in a sort of toast, and with a smile declared, "And that's how we do that! It's always nice to have the President of the company on your side."

"So, no more Hendreik?", asked Eben.

"Well, not in a bothersome way. Not starting tomorrow."

The next day, Carrie drove downtown, waiting until early afternoon, long enough for Williamson to complete his one-on-one with Hendreik. If she could only catch Hendreik right out of the meeting, it would heighten the effect and give him no time to worm his way around it. Surprisingly, she was shown right into his empty office. She spent her time re-emphasizing to herself why she hadn't bothered to bring Leon. If Hendreik was to capitulate, he would do so more readily with no other witnesses to see it - especially those in the industry.

At that last thought the door opened and Hendreik entered. He revealed nothing. He strode casually to his desk, cool and nonchalant. But then, that was Hendreik.

"Miss Ralston. The usual pleasure."

"Let's cut the crap, Hendreik", she shot back. "I've got a list of errands for you. Each item is marked, 'Very important' and 'ASAP'. First, you will return the album to its original state. Second, you will destroy the master copies of your add-ons. Third, you will approve my band for the tour in writing. Oh, let's see, is there anything else? Oh yes. The original album cover is the one we'll use. I guess that concludes this meeting."

Hendreik smiled a half-smile, possibly of resignation, but a certain gleam came into his eye as well. "Is that all?", he asked. "You are not going to add an, 'Or else'?"

The bravado in the face of defeat puzzled her, but she decided to see it through. "Or else," she continued, feeling somewhat less comfortable, "you can count me out. Find some other lackey to hawk your third rate songs."

"Ah. So there it is. The ultimatum. Well, Miss Ralston, believe me when I say, it is immaterial to us whether you participate in 'hawking' the album or not. However, I feel compelled, for your sake alone, to point out a few...salient factors. Since you are, 'cutting the crap', as you say, perhaps you will allow me to do the same." Hendreik rose, went to a cabinet, and slowly poured himself a drink from a silver decanter. He turned slightly as if about to ask her if she wished the same, but caught himself, replaced the stopper, and sat back against the cabinet. Drink in hand, he went on. "Of course you may opt out. You are not our slave. If you do opt out, you will be sued by us for the cost of production of the album, plus the expenses for the tour, plus lost profits from the album and the tour, plus indemnification to us for suits by the promoters of the tour."

Carrie stood and headed for the door with, "We'll see", tossed over her shoulder.

"But don't you wish to hear the rest?"

She halted and turned back, arms crossed, head tilted, and with what she hoped was a look of invincibility on her face.

"You signed your first contract with us some four years ago", he continued. "As an unknown, final say in song selection was given to us, not only on the album, but in any public performance. You signed a replacement contract on the same terms after one year, for a substantial sum based on a percentage of revenue from albums, concerts and promotional materials, for an additional seven years, with a minimum one album per year guarantee. In short, for the next four years, give or take, should you proceed on this course, you will not produce albums, you will not perform, and you will have no income. Given the extent of the lawsuits, I suspect you will lose everything."

Carrie had completely paled. In a meek voice she managed, "I have my residuals."

"Actually, future residuals are forfeited to us as compensation in the event of a breach of the guarantee, as damages. Of course, the breach would have to be established in court. But the residuals would be held until the question was decided, which could take years."

"Those are my songs. They were left...."

"Certainly you own them. But the rights are assigned for the duration of the contract. Your contract is designed to reward you generously, as long as you co-operate in what's best for us all. Go ahead. Have your attorneys confirm this. Considering everything, however", he added with a smirk, "You may wish to limit how much you spend on a retainer."

Carrie felt unable to breathe. She somehow willed her body to begin to move through the door. As she did so and left, she heard Hendreik's final words, a million miles away.

"Look at the positive, Miss Ralston. If you choose to co-operate, you have my word, you may have your album cover."

As she made her way down the hallway, she had one sole purpose: to get out without seeing anyone and never come back. She rounded the corner to the lobby and came face to face with Bill Williamson. Tanned, smiling and looking even more inflated than ususal, he stopped before her, placing his hands on her shoulders.

"Carrie. Good to see you. All the confusion worked out I trust?"

"I think everything's perfectly clear", she replied quietly.

"Good. You know what I always say? What's good for the Company is good for us all. Well, good to see you Carrie."

With that, he sidestepped her and continued down the hall in one smooth, dismissive motion. But she didn't care. She instantly moved on, through the lobby and down the stairs to her parking level, stopping for a second only once, when she reached her parking spot. Then she jumped into her car and roared away, sparing little rubber, and leaving far behind Melanie's silver Sebring convertible in the space beside.

Eben looked up just as a slender figure emerged from the tunnel out into the open air. The man, hands in pockets, carried on to the edge overlooking the sea, paused for a few moments, staring out at it, then turned. Giving Eben a nod of recognition and a smile, he went over to the bar.

"I heard you were working here. It's a good thing, you know. I'll take a beer", he said, and sat down.

"Haven't seen you around for a while, Zack", replied Eben.

"Oh, I've been around. Never been here much without Carrie. Never been down there." He tipped the bottle towards the deck below, took a gulp, and winked. "Thought I'd come in one last time. One for the road."

Eben gave a slight frown, then a slow nod of understanding. "Where to?"

'Mississippi. Gulf coast. The boys and me, that's where we're from. We came out together. Fifteen years ago now. They're still back at the house, packin' up. Course, there ain't much, but gettin' them to do anything is like trying to herd fleas. I guess that's why I'm boss." He laughed.

"I never did meet the rest."

"And you wouldn't, would you. Carrie'd never let them near her place - said they weren't housebroken. For the most part she was right." He laughed again and shook his head. "But man, she was good to us. We were half-starved when she found us. Then it was top of the line everything, first class tour bus, hotels. I guess 'cause money-wise she kinda came from the same place, you know? Musically, it wasn't really our thing. We were more Gulf and Western, but somehow it all seemed to work. This new stuff though", he rolled his eyes. "I'd pay money not to have to play it." He really paused, and his head tilted slightly. "Quite a ride while it lasted."

"You don't seem too upset that it's over", noted Eben.

"Oh hell no. Are you kiddin'? I'll let you in on a little secret. We weren't fired. We quit. Taped one session, took one look at the boys and went over and told that son-of-a-bitch Hendreik where he could shove it. Didn't tell Carrie 'cause I figured it would spur her on. Oh, what the hell. He was going to fire us anyway."

Eben smiled. "Obviously you weren't planning on sticking around."

"Well. You know, for four years we didn't precisely sell our souls to that devil Hendreik, but we sure as hell rented them out for a while. It was worth it. Good music, good times, made a pile of money."

"And now?"

"Well, I know of this little place, holds maybe a hundred and fifty. Right on the water. Little marina, ping pong table outside. We're gonna give 'em what they want for it, and we'll be the house band. Friday and Saturday nights. Get back to what we're supposed to do. The rest of the time you'll find me fishin' the surf." He drained the rest of the beer, stood up and stretched, and threw a bill on the bar. "Well, I'd better get back and see if they got that truck even half loaded."

"Can you wait around for Carrie? She shouldn't be too long."

Zack took a long look over his shoulder at the ocean, and another at the floor.

"I don't think I will. There's not much I can.... Just tell her... tell her to look us up next time she's down our way. And tell her... thanks."

"Well, take care then." offered Eben.

"You take it easy," replied Zack, shaking the hand given him. "You're a good thing for her right now, you know. She needs you. She don't know it yet, but she will." He began to walk towards the tunnel, then stopped and turned. "You know, she don't have to know where she's going, so long as she knows when she gets there." He turned again, and with a final glance at the water and a wave of his hand, he disappeared.

Carrie's initial reaction to the meeting was to go through a rapid-fire inventory of her immediate resources. She desperately needed to counteract the numbness and disconsolation she now felt. Leon was the principle choice, but she doubted he would have any better ideas than she. The lawyers would have plenty of time for review - years even. And the appointment of Eben as adviser, now that push had come to shove, seemed more whimsical than anything else. As he himself had said, he knew nothing of the music industry. Right now she needed a different perspective.

Carrie drove on aimlessly, but the further away she travelled from the company building, the more vague and diffused her thoughts seemed to become. Her breathing became faster and her vision noticeably blurred. In order to recover she needed to become centred once again. She remembered her foray into consciousness classes with Melanie, but recalled that upon starting, the Instructor had invited them to, "Imagine you're by the ocean". Now, as before, she ended up heading for her beach.

She was in the door of her house before the gates had stopped closing, leaving the Lotus hissing and sighing in the courtyard. Past a half-asleep and bewildered Sadie, she pushed out the door and across the deck, only to be stopped cold at the top of the stairs. She was halted not by a sight or a sound but a feeling, or more precisely, the lack thereof. She seemed ironically conscious of being frozen in a vacuous state - intellectually aware, but totally disconnected: like viewing a live street scene through a surveillance camera. She could see the waves coming in, the sun overhead, the various people meandering by from time to time, but felt no immediate experience of it. She knew she should smell the salt air, feel the warmth of the sun, hear the laughter of the children, but couldn't. She knew she should be rejuvenated by it, but wasn't. Nor could she propel herself forward. Down below was what she needed, that lifeblood of her soul that she had always relied upon, that had never failed to succour her, and that she was now discerning was gone. For what she knew to be hours she stood there, transfixed, waiting for some indication that she was wrong, some minute digression from everything that her senses proved to her, afraid to move forward to be proven right. Finally, lacking the strength to endure it further, she slowly took two careful steps backwards, then turned to re-enter the house, forsaking the sunset altogether.

CHAPTER 12

The room became quiet as the resonance died out, first in the instruments themselves, then in their electronic manifestation, and finally in the stage floor as felt through Carrie's feet, and reverberating on through her body. An odd, all-encompassing silence followed, even more vacant due to the absence of the thunderous applause one would normally hope for, and even expect. As a result, no one moved for an unnatural dozen seconds, until finally a few roadies in the back offered some token clapping, and broke the spell.

"Then Carrie acknowledges first Melanie who bows and exits stage left then the band who bow and exit stage left then Carrie bows and exits stage right then returns and bows again and exits stage right. No further encores. Thank you everyone. Sound check is at five p.m. tomorrow. Show is at eight."

It was the voice of the producer droning at them electronically as it had for several days. He had been hand-picked by Hendreik, and Carrie had long since forgotten his name, much less where he was situated in the darkened fore-front to the temporary platform on which the rehearsals had been held. This, of course, assumed he was actually still there. It had occurred to her that they may have been listening to pre-recorded directives all along, all engineered and cued by Hendreik, the self-proclaimed Executive Producer, likely in some money saving scheme, but above all in a further bid for even more control. But it really didn't matter.

Carrie gave a perfunctory wave to the band as they departed. She could be diplomatic when required. After all, there was nothing wrong with them. They were good musicians. All week long they never missed a beat, or changed one, or improvised, or added a note for that matter. If this was the new music, she would show them she could thrive in it. If this was the new business, she would show them she could succeed. So what if it had no soul. It really didn't matter.

Hendreik, she knew, was somewhere out in the darkness as well, as he had been all along. Overseeing. Domineering. Predatory. For the first few days she had avoided him like the plague, and when that wasn't possible, immediately became overly deferential so as not to reveal her intense detestation and thereby heighten his victory. Gradually, however, the facade became the reality. There was no use fighting it - he had won. It didn't matter.

Carrie's natural inclination was to proceed stage left, contrary to instructions. It would be a minimal achievement in a tiny battle at best, but would have at least shown some spirit. As she looked across the room her energy failed her, and it was only spotting Leon in that direction that ultimately pulled her forward.

As she approached, his hands remained in his pockets, and his mouth in a frown, but he began to shift his weight nervously from foot to foot, looking anxiously around the room, avoiding her gaze. She stopped, facing him, her arms straight down at her front, clasping her hands together.

"So?"

Leon stopped his swaying and looked at her.

"It was...good", he replied. And managed a slight upturn in the corners of his mouth, while the rest of the frown contrarily remained. "I think it will work."

She began to try to gauge his sincerity, but recalled that Leon was rarely ever insincere, and left it at that. As for herself, what she was sure was a complete deadpan expression would likely suffice for a reply. She noticed Leon's expression change as he looked over her shoulder, minutely rolled his eyes, and found something in the corner of the room to fix his attention. Then she felt Eben beside her.

Leon closed his eyes and rubbed between them for a moment. "Your car should be outside by now," he mentioned. "I'll see you tonight". He headed for the door.

Carrie turned to Eben and noticed he had brought her jacket and purse, which he proceeded to help her on with and hand over. She gave him the faintest trace of a smile.

"Well?"

"Your voice is even more beautiful in person," he remarked. "But I guess that makes sense."

It had been the first time he had heard her sing live, and the first of the rehearsals he had attended, which was at her insistence, wanting to wait until the product was in its finished form.

"And the music?"

"It's fine," Eben shrugged.

She tilted her head and raised her eyebrows at him.

"I mean, I don't have much to compare it to," he continued. "The stuff in the middle sounds just like your albums. It's amazing how they can do that. The rest is...okay."

She sighed and they turned to walk to the exit. "Idiot-breath over there insisted on book-ending the show with all the new material," she proclaimed, jerking her thumb back towards the darkness. "Six songs to start. Six songs to finish. I don't think it's a good idea. But it doesn't matter."

They halted, Eben looked at her quizzically for a moment, then said, "I'll check on the car," and departed.

Carrie sighed again and turned to see Melanie before her with an urgent, though curiously not in the least pleading, look on her face.

"Carrie, I've got to talk to you - life or death!" She paused, and displayed as much of a thoughtful look as Carrie had ever seen her muster. "I've been considering sort of an image change. You know, I'm kind of in a rut."

"You have an image?"

"Well, Hendreik thinks it's a good idea. What do you think about, 'Virginia White'?"

"Hendriek? You listen to Hendreik?"

"Sure! You really should spend more time with him. He's really an amazing man."

"Yeah. He's amazing all right. You realize no one will connect you to your credits on the album, or any of them for that matter."

"That's all right. Hendreik says it shouldn't make a difference. So from now on, Virginia, okay?"

"Sure, whatever," Carrie replied, and watched Melanie wink and move away. But she found herself confronted by something she had never experienced under the same circumstances, and could never have predicted. Nothing. There was no one in line, no one asking questions, no one wanting anything. She felt like the last person on earth. She glanced around the now empty room.

Long, low, windowless, dark, airless, gloomy, ceiling-tiled, upholstered satin chairs with little tables and lamps along the sides, and more chairs in front of the platform. It reminded her of a funeral home. She hated funeral homes. Fitting, she thought.

Eben appeared, and together they strode out into the waning light of post-sunset. Before her was a massive black limousine, probably designed to seat twelve, and a driver dressed in black. Fitting. As they climbed inside she noticed the closed glass partition between the driver and them, intended for privacy, rendered somewhat superfluous first by the sheer length of the vehicle, then by the fact that not much was being said. She sat, arms folded, knee crossed and vision directed away from Eben. She had no wish for conversation and had no intention of initiating one, but could certainly think ill of him until he did. At last he spoke.

"Why are you doing this?", he asked.

"What do you mean?"

"This is not you. It's not your kind of music. Even I can tell that. You don't have to do it."

"We've been over this before", she sighed. "I'm not spending the next four years of my life not singing, worried about losing everything I've got fighting so I can sing, when all I have to do is put up with these ass-holes for four more years and then I'm done with them. I know it's like Purgatory but I'm going to see it through."

"But it's not a certainty you can't sing."

'Sure, it can be argued - restraint of trade or something. But that could take years to decide and cost a fortune. And even if I win, which is very doubtful, I'd have nothing to sing - the songs are all tied up. The bottom line is I signed a contract and I'm paying for my own stupidity."

"You know your heart isn't in it."

"Look," she lashed out, "not everybody gets to just free-wheel around the globe, doing whatever the hell comes to hand. Some of us have dreams and aspirations. We conceive them, develop and nurture them, and we stick with them. We don't just run away when the going gets tough."

She regretted it the moment she said it, but she wasn't going to take it back. There was a long pause, then came Eben's voice, quiet and un-emotional.

"I'd like to see a copy of the contract, if it's okay with you."

"So, what? You're going to be a lawyer now?", she retorted, with more than just a hint of maliciousness. "We've got lawyers on top of lawyers looking at this thing."

"I just want to know what you're up against."

She considered. "Fine. I'll have Leon get you one."

After another pause, Eben quietly and almost casually added, "I care what happens to you."

Carrie didn't respond. She didn't doubt what Eben had said. She knew she was being hard on him, and directing her frustrations his way. She knew she cared about him in return. But right now, she just couldn't compel herself to feel it.

They might as well not have gone home, Carrie thought to herself. They were situated in the limousine in the exact same positions as before. Nothing much had been said between them in the interim, and she hadn't had a speck to eat. They had merely changed clothes, hers from black t-shirt, jeans and low shoes to black silk top, leather jacket and pants, and high-heeled boots, not necessarily conducive to yacht-going but what the hell.

The car slowed, was waved through some very anal-looking security guards, and began to crest a hill. Slowly the glare beyond began to take form: impossibly long, two decks above, at least two below, gigantic black-tinted windows, a helicopter pad on the stern from which one was just departing and another set to land, bringing god knows who from god knows where. Incredibly sleek, it looked to Carrie exactly like a giant dust-buster on water. As they drove up she noticed the multitude of banners proclaiming that 'The Edwards Conglomerate Welcomes You', and wondered whether anyone either believed it was sincere, or even bothered to judge its sincerity at all. They were resplendent in gaudy green and yellow, the corporate colours. The ship's hull was green and it was trimmed with yellow as well. It was named the 'Edwardian'.

They stopped in front of a long green carpet leading to a fixed stairway and up to the open deck of the ship. Eben gave her a questioning look.

"Haven't you heard?," she replied. "I have a new benefactor. I've never met him, of course, but I had about as much to say about that as anything else, including this launch party. Get ready to smile."

They made their way through a polite throng, obviously

hand-picked in advance, with the occasional flash of a camera and offering the requisite applause. As they reached the top of the stairs someone grabbed her arm, and she recognized one of Hendreik's countless but nameless yes-people.

"Good evening Miss Ralston. First we'll be going in for a photo-op with Mr. Edwards and Mr. Williamson, and the official welcome. Then there will be a meet and greet with the guests. Then we'll have you autograph the album for any of the guests who want one."

She was pulled into a large room, doors and windows open on three sides, crammed full of people with more peering in from the deck, all attention rivetted on one man, who she presumed was Edwards. He was about fifty-five, medium build, medium height, well toned and tanned, salt and pepper immaculately-trimmed hair. God, she thought, do they stamp these things out in a factory somewhere? He was just finishing his dissertation.

"...of course, I've never been out on her. Who would have the time for that? I just have her moved from port to port when I want to have one of these little get-togethers." Everyone laughed obediently, and he glanced in her direction. "Carrie! There you are! Come on over here. Ladies and Gentlemen, a great friend of mine and the backbone of a terrific partnership, the woman of the hour and the woman of my dreams, and many others here I'll bet," (more laughter), "Carrie Ralston."

She was whisked to his side, amid more perfunctory applause, received a big hug and kiss, and with flashes going off and Bill Williamson suddenly appearing close on her other arm, she became the meat in an almost suffocating corporate sandwich. After indeterminable minutes, Edwards shouted out, "That should look good in this month's newsletter," (laughter again). Carrie feigned an obliging smile. "Emile, has the last chopper landed?", he continued. "Then on with the lights!"

A glow filled the sky and with an "Ooooh!", of admiration the crowd hurried aft to see the laser show projecting green and gold stars into the dark, cloudy sky. Carrie took the opportunity to slip forward on the harbour side of the ship, unnoticed, for which she was grateful. But she couldn't escape feeling like some cog in a machine that was temporarily switched off and therefore forgotten - one that every-one took for granted unless it suddenly stopped working like it was supposed to. She felt Eben's presence beside her and his hand lightly on the small of her back. They walked on further.

"Who are all those people?", he asked.

She sighed. "I don't know. Nosy celebrities. Potential investors." She chuckled. "They haven't even heard the album yet - it doesn't get released until tomorrow. Boy are they going to be disappointed." Just then some indistinct music came over the ship's sound system which took her a moment to recognize as a cut from the album. She winced, and continued, "I hardly know anyone."

They came upon an open room, encamped in the corner of which was Melanie in the highest cut dress Carrie had ever seen, sparkling red, long-sleeved and low-cut in front, gleefully engulfed by three males, somewhat recognizable as local pro athletes. She saw Carrie at once, and with a gleaming smile, sent to her signals of two fingers on her right hand, and three on her left. Carrie returned what smile she could force in response, not caring how genuine it looked, and they moved on.

"What was that all about?", queried Eben.

"Didn't you know? New name, new image, new life. It's that easy."

"Hmmm", he responded doubtfully. "I think she'll need more help than that. A rose by any other name...."

She contemplated for a moment, then turned to him. "I think I'd like something to drink."

"I think I can manage that", he replied, and moved off further forward.

Carrie stepped to the railing and took hold. Behind her she could feel the multitudes starting to return, apparently bored with the light show, but not yet convinced sufficiently that the meet and greet had begun in order to start approaching her. As their numbers increased and the sterile music droned on, a terrible reality began to sink in - of the impossible position in which she had been placed. She had shouldered great responsibility before, but never with virtually no control. Her hand began to shake so she grasped the railing tighter. She began to feel a panic within her.

Just then Eben appeared and she was handed a large glass of wine. She gave him a small thank you, then turned to peer over the side. The reflection of the laser stars were twinkling over the slightly rolling water. Seen through that medium, they seemed almost tantalizing. Out of the corner of her eye she spied Hendreik's yes-person coming forward to find her.

"Eben, could you be a dear and find me a tissue? I think I saw some in that first room we were in." She offered as sweet and imploring a look as she could manage. He looked at her blankly, then gave a slight nod and moved back aft. Carrie watched him go, then tossed the wine overboard, set the glass on the railing, and hurried off to follow Eben's previous path forward. She halted only once, when she saw a man come up some stairs from the lower deck, looking somewhat energized and rubbing his nose. Carrie hesitated for a moment. She had only ever tried speed, once before, and a little pot, but they weren't for her. So she quickly carried on and, bypassing a crowded table of food, eventually found the bar. She was ecstatic to find a punch-bowl with a little card reading, 'Planters Punch'. It was assured her glass could keep being filled and refilled with no one the wiser. She quickly downed one glass, then after looking casually around, downed another. She filled a third, and nonchalantly began to drift away from the table when she noticed Leon in the corner, with a large glass of whiskey, neat, now almost empty, quietly getting drunk. She went to him.

He looked up at her, and smiled a tiny smile. "Don't worry," he said. "It's not failure if it's success."

Carrie sombrely studied him for a moment, then drained her glass and left to fill it again. She had just replaced the ladle when Hendreik's yes-person caught up with her.

What followed was round after round of the ship, meeting endless people, none of whom she knew, with meaningless banter becoming more unintelligible each time she paused to refill her glass by the punch table, which she manoeuvred to do frequently, by pretending at every opportunity to recognize someone she either wanted to meet or re-meet, whose sole redeeming qualities were actually their immediately proximity to its location. The noise, the close quarters, the suffocating sameness of the music which she now vaguely perceived to be no longer her own, all combined to create a dizziness she couldn't shake. She began to feel an intense, livid resentment of her situation - all of it - and to search for an object to vent it on. She suddenly spied Hendreik across the room, and, breaking away, began to stumble towards him. Whether it was the ten planters punches, the lack of food since breakfast, the totality of the stress of everything, the innate roll of the ship, or the utter revulsion with which she regarded him - she would never determine the precise source of the vengeance that was about to spew forth.

Carrie woke in a haze, but was vaguely able to discern, there in the darkness, that the bed that was spinning beneath her was her own. She reached down and found that she was wearing a long t-shirt, but that her bra had been removed. Eben must have done that, she thought. She smiled a little to herself. That was alright. But in a flash she searched lower and, relieved to find her panties where she had left them, sank back to her pillow where, despite everything, she collapsed in a state of mildly contented exhaustion.

CHAPTER 13

What awakened Carrie first were the series of freight trains roaring through her room, one after another after another. This drew her attention to the searchlight directly and unceasingly trained on her face. As she turned to its source, firecrackers went off in a cacophonous staccato. She gradually improved to a state of semi-consciousness, and somewhat remotely discerned that she had been enduring the sound of the waves outside, a tiny sliver of light between the drapes, and her hair crinkling against the pillow. She turned back, and an incredible surge of nausea convinced her that future movement in this lifetime would not be advisable. She lay there, and while examining with her tongue each nodule of the extra-coarse sandpaper which the inside of her mouth had become, had a long period to contemplate her fate. For a while she was afraid she might die. Then she was afraid she might live.

At last her overwhelming thirst gave a small glimmer of purpose to her existence, and mustering the minimal strength she possessed, rose to get out of bed. A shock of agony impaled her head on her first step, as though she had stomped on the raw nerves of her brain. With her forearm shielding her eyes, and using what little memory that had survived, she wobbled down the hallway into the living room and collapsed on the sofa, a pillow over her head, which promptly exploded beneath. She heard the booming voice of Eben calling out.

"I've got you some cold water, a bottle of aspirin, and a little bit of bread."

"Uhhhh," she responded, from somewhere far away.

"But I have bad news for you," he continued. "It's almost two o'clock."

Carrie stood alone in the middle of her dressing room in high heels and a knee-length party dress, black lace and black sequins over black. Eyes closed, she rubbed her aching temples and groaned. Maybe more water and aspirin, she thought. Even her hair hurt.

They had arrived in the funeral car a few hours before to the sight of the towering entertainment complex adorned in uninterrupted advertisements of green and yellow, looking for all the world like a colossal, domed, jellied fruit salad. She had struggled through the sound check, wondering where Eben had vanished to, until she spotted him in a seat some distance away, engrossed in the copy of the contract that had been provided for him.

Now, after hours of meet and greets, and having shooed everyone out of the room, she had rushed to turn off the speakers. They had been spewing endless, introductory, mind-numbing samples of up-and-coming company talents to her and anyone else who had nowhere to run to, particularly the crowd assembling downstairs, whose presence she could feel within herself, even from that far away. Poor bastards, she thought.

A knock came and Melanie appeared, closing the door behind her.

"I know this is probably a bad time, but I thought you should know as soon as possible. Hendreik's offered me a contract. Isn't it great? He says he's never heard a voice like mine. And he says the biggest plus is that I can dance as well as sing."

"You can dance?"

"Well, you know, I used to shake my booty pretty good in parades and stuff when I was a kid. My album will be out in three weeks."

"Three weeks?"

"Yes! Isn't it great? The tracks are all pre-recorded. All I have to do is record my part. Then it's off on a tour, opening for somebody or other. My coming-out party is next week. But don't worry, Hendreik's got a replacement already prepping to come in and do my bit in the show." Her face sobered, and she came forward with her hand outstretched. "I want to thank you for your assistance and wish you the best of luck in the future," she offered, and went to leave the room.

"Wait," cried Carrie. Melanie stopped and turned back. Carrie opened her mouth to say something, closed it again, then, "Never mind. Just...good luck."

With a smile and a wink, Melanie skipped on out.

Carrie stood for a while, staring blankly through the wall, with no thoughts she could hang on to. She heard a noise behind her, and saw Eben enter the room and walk to her.

"Are you all right?", he asked.

"Fine", she replied, "Why shouldn't I be?", and looked around unsuccessfully for something to occupy her hands.

"Just...." Then, glancing at the contract in his hand, "I think I found something in here. Listen to this." He flipped through some pages, then went on. "'The Company shall have complete authority over all third-party generated materials. All materials as supplied aforesaid are subject to the consent of the Company in its absolute discretion in regard to, but not limited to, selection for recording, performance and airplay, scheduling of concerts, promotion,' and so on. I can't see anything in here about songs not written by other people," he concluded excitedly. "Obviously nobody ever expected that you might...." He glanced up and was halted by a mournful look on her face. She stood silently, one arm straight down at her side, the other crossed over, hugging it, looking at anything but him. He regarded her for a moment. "Have you ever...?"

Carrie quietly took just enough steps to turn herself away.

"I tried. A long time ago. A few efforts," she laughed mildly. "I've never actually sung them. They weren't very...."

She paused and bowed her head. "They weren't like his. He was supportive, but...."

Her voice trailed off. She looking upwards in a vain attempt to stem the tears that were threatening, her arms straight at her side, fists clenched in the effort.

"Vocal interpretation is a perfectly legitimate form of self-expression", she continued in a voice that was now quivering.

"I realize that. But it doesn't necessarily tell your story. It doesn't set you free."

A torrent of tears came rushing from her. For a moment she wiped away what she could, then turned back to face him.

"Why do you try to make me give up all I have when you give me nothing to take its place?", Carrie lashed out. She hid her face in her hands and turned away, and the tears came again. He went to her and began to put his hand on her arm but she pulled it free. For moments she stood there feeling her muscles stiffen, and her heart grow numb. Then, looking up, she went on coldly, "Maybe it's time for you to move on."

He studied her, his grey eyes never leaving hers. "Is that what you want?"

She contemplated him in return, trying to imagine him gone, trying to imagine him staying. Her mind could take hold of none of it. She turned her head to sniffle, and wipe away a final tear. Shaking her head slightly, she replied, "Let's not talk about it now. We'll talk about it tonight."

A knock came at the door and an anonymous head poked

through. "Miss Ralston," it announced, "ready in five minutes." Eben continued looking at Carrie for a moment, then turned and brushed past, out of the room.

Carrie crept along the dark passageway, airless and confining, perhaps primarily because of the lines of countless so-called well wishers, faceless and blurry, babbling incessantly and incoherently, and reaching out to grasp her as she passed by. They seemed to hang over her from each side as she struggled to follow the path of the unknown guide in front of her. Her headache had not receded, and as they moved forward it became paired with a dizziness, intense but diffused, almost like she was looking at things upside down. Part of her vision to the left seemed to become fragmented and disappeared, as in a kaleidoscope - the figures in front of her drawn down and out of sight ten feet away, only to rise up again as she came directly alongside. She gripped the back of the jacket of the guide and closed her eyes.

As she listened to the horrible, unrecognizable, inescapable renderings of the sound system ahead of her, she thought she could detect out of the engulfing morass the familiar gut-tightening which signalled the presence of a concert to be performed. But the feeling became gradually though irrefutably replaced by another. As her thoughts leapt forward to what lay ahead, the naked impact of her uncertainty, her physical state, and her lack of conviction melded into the reality of her destiny, and she began to panic.

As she was halted at the side of the stage, she began to frantically search in vain for Eben, then to resent him for bringing out this desperate weakness in her. In a state of almost morbid terror, she peered out to face a vast mass of indistinguishable forms, alternately in pitch black then glaring light, and driven to a peak of excitement by the unceasing flashes of an overwhelmingly spectacular green and yellow laser light show above their heads. She recoiled and turned away, only to be met by Leon, looking paler than she had ever seen him despite the lurid green and yellow glare reflection on his face.

He avoided her gaze for a moment, the turned to look her in the eyes. He managed a little smile.

"Don't worry," he offered. "Just do your best. Just try to get through it." And he was gone.

Sudden blackness and the close-following eruption of live music signalled that the band had taken the stage, catching Carrie off-guard. Before she could prepare herself, the voice of an announcer blasted throughout the building.

"The Edwards Conglomerate welcomes you! This is your invitation to get ready, to hold on and experience the premier singing talent of our time! Her four releases have been certified multi-platinum! She's a multiple award winner! And Edwards Conglomerate has her! Edwards Conglomerate has brought you a multitude of new and vibrant products and services, and now we are proud to bring you, Carrie Ralston!"

An inhuman squall of pandemonium burst forth, driven by an even more intense tidal-wave of laser lights. Carrie grasped the sides of her head in her hands for a moment in one last attempt to steady herself, then strode forward, waving and feigning a smile as she went. She reached the microphone and began to sing. The material was not second nature to her, but her instinct and professionalism pushed her flatly onward. Abruptly she was swallowed up by a multitude of green and yellow spotlights, and the laser show started again, completely unexpected, and probably purposely planned so by Hendreik. She carried on, her hands tightly wound around the microphone and stand, and her eyes closed more than was usual, like someone who had set off on a terrifying carnival ride, too late to turn back, and now could only endure it, seemingly excruciating and interminable. At last the song finished and the complex was pitched into darkness. A few seconds of applause issued forth, less vibrant than before and for the most part merely polite, and the next song commenced immediately.

On it droned, accompanied by more lights, until she began to notice an unearthly squeal around her. It continued on as she looked pleadingly towards the sound technician, but with no relief. The sound seemed to penetrate her - defiling her just as it corrupted the music. Then Carrie's voice was gone. She knew in her head she was still singing, but was obliterated by everything around. The cruel ineffectualness went on and on, until, with spasms of static, she returned, but much diminished from before. She bolstered herself for a second with as much energy as she could muster, and was horrified to perceive that the sound system was now back to normal. The deficiency was in her. In despair she signalled the band to finish the song early, but as she stopped, they did not, and it carried on to its end without her.

The applause was wholly token now and marked by an undercurrent of unsettled grumbling. Carrie felt her throat begin to close, and started gasping for air. But then she remembered where they were in the set, and knowing she could find refuge in something basic and familiar, she started to relax.

"I'd like to introduce you...", she began, but as she looked up to address the crowd, she was cut down by the sight of Borland, standing several rows back, fixing his eyes on her with a glare of sadistic pleasure. For endless seconds she was held. Her imploring eyes sought his for mercy, but to no avail. Only the cat-calls of the audience finally shook her free, and she began, hesitatingly, again. "I...want to...introduce...uh...the band."

An intuitive feeling of relief flooded over her, and she turned to her friends. "On lead guitar, Za...."

The blank stare of the strangers before her made her breath choke off. In an instant she was down to the floor, scrambling to find the sheet she had placed there during sound check. She retrieved it and mechanically began to rhyme off the names, to virtual silence, until, with one final sigh, she concluded, "And on backup vocals, Melanie Black."

In the quiet she heard the gasp behind her, and the reality of her mistake stabbed her like a knife. She whirled to face Melanie, and was confronted by her anguished face, a combination of hurt, betrayal and anger, reflected through the tears now beginning to form. Carrie stared at first as if in shock, then began to beg Melanie with her eyes for a sign of forgiveness, which didn't come.

"Uh, I mean, Virginia White...now...who will be releasing her own very first album. Soon. Good for her."

Finally, sometime in the silence that followed, she motioned the band to begin the next song. This they did, but when it soon became apparent that Melanie wasn't joining in, Carrie found her focus draining away. Out of her memory came Leon's deduction that Hendreik really wanted her to fail. She felt herself sliding inextricably into the abyss of the satisfaction of his scheme. She began to scan the corporate boxes at the top of the complex, knowing he was somewhere up there in the darkness, looming over her, controlling her, owning her very soul. She stumbled on a line, then missed a few words, then stopped singing completely, as if she had lost her voice forever. The yells from the audience increased as the music petered out and died. The yells turned to boos, but Carrie faced them as one would a public stoning, taking in the full brunt of the indignation from each and every source. She stood still, head bowed, hanging on to the microphone stand, making no attempt to stem her tears which now flowed freely. Then, after one last look at the mob before her, she turned and bolted off the stage, through a back exit and out into the night, pursued by an even more angry chorus of boos, her eradication complete.

Chaos followed. The confusion was fuelled by the yells and screams of the crowd which began to turn on itself, and then on the security which attempted to calm it. The band, the roadies, and the hangers-on wandered aimlessly around the stage and behind, in a daze seemingly perpetuated by obliteration of purpose.

Within a moment, however, Eben and Leon found themselves face to face at the exit through which Carrie had vanished. They both pulled up and eyed each other: Eben with a questioning look and Leon with one of distrust. Then Leon looked slightly downward, back to Eben again, gave a slight nod, and without a word Eben was through the door and gone.

Eben stepped cautiously out onto the deck and to the railing, the shoes left strewn on the landing and the door slightly ajar apparently sufficient clues. The night was incredibly clear but moonless, giving the countless stars more intensity than usual. Through the warm night, the ocean could be heard but not seen. He proceeded quickly down the stairs, then paused to carefully scan the beach.

The waves were coming in with a gentle consistency, their small, white crests now visible through the blackness. At one point a break in their line could be discerned, and he hurried towards it. He stopped ten feet short, close enough to make out the huddled form of Carrie, kneeling just past the water's edge, so that the folds of her dress appeared to merge with the sea. Her face was buried in her hands and she was sobbing convulsively. Before her, awash in the surf and out of her reach, was the broken and still-entwined form of the lifeless seagull.

CHAPTER 14

The water was no more than tepid, and the onset of slight shivering had begun. But this was where she must be. Carrie felt it. Marooned not on land, not fully in the water, she couldn't go forward, but she couldn't go back. Not ever. The sea surrounded her, soaking what it could reach, enveloping her in its sand, which rose up to her like the pedestal of a mournful statue. It pulled her irresistibly downward as she waited in the darkness. Waited for nothing, the nothingness of welcome oblivion, her hands shielding her tight-shut eyes against any remnants of the world that might try to penetrate the huddled little ball that was all that was left of her. Images plagued her, haunting one moment, terrifying the next, but no thoughts, no ideas, no solutions. Only an innate will to be forever gone.

She felt a hand grasp her arm, then a second hand the other. Unstartled, she slowly raised her head. The mild, continuous roar of the surf reached her first. Then, as vision returned, she made out before her a face, sad and concerned, illuminated by the stars alone, and slowly revealed to be that of Eben.

"Carrie", he said softly. "Come with me. It'll be all right."

She made no reply, but felt his arms move under hers and pull her to her feet. She teetered there for a second, and he caught her, her face thrust upwards where she glimpsed the trace of a smile he offered her. Then he picked her up out of the water, and carried her to the beach. She melded into him as the sand had to her, arms wrapped around his neck, face buried in it, cocooned within the warmth and the smell of spice. At length he stopped and she felt herself turning in his arms to face him, then slowly sliding down his body to rest on her feet. He immediately supported her from behind, and led her forward. He had done that before, she vaguely remembered, but as she turned slightly to look down the beach, she could not grasp just when it had been.

They came to the stairs and started to climb. All fear had left her. All thoughts about before or after. She lost herself in letting go of everything except the man she could feel solidly beside her. As they reached the deck, Eben guided her to the door and stopped. She felt him reach up, take hold of the zipper to her dress, and gradually pull it down. The dress, full of sand and seawater, dropped to the deck, and he took her hand to help her step out of it, like a little wind-up doll. She waited passively while he removed his soaking-wet shoes, then he led her into the house. Across the landing they went, and down the hall to her bedroom. There they faced each other, she in her wet underwear, he in his clothes, almost equally as wet from carrying her. She studied his face. His eyes, intense and as large as she'd ever seen them, never left hers, seeming to study her in return. Was she really so hard to read? She called out to him with her eyes. No. She could not go back. Not ever.

Eben finally looked slightly down and to the side, then continuing to avert his eyes, he led her forward once again, this time to the bathroom. There he found her a large bath towel and face cloth, placing them on the counter-top. He began to walk past her out of the room, but a catching of his hand by Carrie stopped him. He turned to her, and she looked him in the eyes for a moment. All she could feel was that a part of her stood a few feet away, a chasm that she could no longer endure. She released his hand, then slowly removed first her bra, then her panties. Standing before him, still meeting his eyes, she could feel within herself the totality of her being, and the essence of what she was to become. She went to him, and together they removed his clothes. She moved into his arms, her head resting on his shoulder, her arms clinging to him, her skin awakening to the touch of his.

For endless moments they stood there. A few final sobs escaped her. Then she took hold of his hand once again - she would lead now - and he followed her into the marbled shower room. In the midst of the soft, warm, stream of water, he tenderly caressed her skin with gel, and she his. His fingers moved through her hair, washing it, stroking it. She turned to him, observing his face for a moment, then, placing her hand to the side of it, slowly traced down his neck and chest, along his abdomen and hip to his thigh. She moved forward and they kissed deeply, completely. The utter sweetness of it brought a tear briefly to her eye. The thought of time lost came to her, but she let it go. The past was gone.

Carrie took Eben's hand once more. They left the shower room and silently towelled each other dry. She led him back into the bedroom, turned down the bed, then facing him and lightly grasping both of his hands, lay back against the pillows, urging him to her with her hands and her eyes. As they lay there together, he began to softly kiss her neck and chest, but she touched his face and he stopped. She kissed him passionately for a while, then pulled slightly back. She wanted those eyes, to gaze at them, to drink them in, to be lost in them. As she did so, she pulled him forward, to become part of her, and she of him, and she was complete.

Carrie lay awake in the soft, early morning light. The muted sound of the waves, and the balmy ocean air, drifted though the open window, and the curtains gently stirred. But everything was new and different. So many thoughts came to mind all at once she hardly knew where to begin. How long had it been since she felt like this? She had hardly remembered what a man's gentle touch felt like. Maybe that was exaggerated, but still it seemed like forever. Maybe it was forever. She thought on it some more. Maybe it was never.

She snuggled in closer to Eben, sleeping quietly beside her, and kissed him on the chest. Why had they waited so long? It seemed ridiculous now, but there's a purpose for everything, she reasoned. Maybe it wouldn't have felt so wonderful before. The recollection of her telling him he should leave, only twelve hours before, came to her, but was so abhorrent to her now, she actually shook her head to rid it from her mind. He stirred slightly, and she froze in order not to wake him further. After a moment she relaxed again, and began to lightly trace her fingers over what part of his body they could reach. She smiled at the realization that they were now lovers, and that it could never be taken away. She began to recount with a delicious self-indulgence all the places he had touched, the spots he had kissed, everywhere their bodies had met. She felt him there still.

Carrie leaned over, left just a trace of a kiss on his lips, then noiselessly slipped out of bed. She donned her robe and tiptoed out the door, returning in a few minutes with a tray of croissants, jam and orange juice, which she placed on the dresser. Just then Eben woke, and lifted his head from the pillow.

"Oh," she exclaimed, "I didn't want to wake you."

He opened his eyes wider to try to shake off his sleepiness. "No time for omelettes?", he asked.

She gave him raised eyebrows but couldn't suppress a smile, then tore off her robe and dove beneath the covers. She rolled on top of him, her breasts pressed flat against his chest, and gave him a long, hard kiss.

"Do you know how many hours I've been waiting to do that?", she playfully demanded.

"Do you know have many weeks I've been wishing you would?", he replied.

She studied his face and her expression sobered for a moment. Then she smiled and kissed him again.

"Hey", he asked between kisses. "Aren't you supposed to be somewhere? Doing something?"

"Nope", she responded, moving down past his ears to his neck. "I called and left a message that I'm okay but that no one's to call or stop by." She halted to look him in the eye. "We can stay here just like this. Forever, if we want to."

"Why would you do that?"

She smiled. "'Cause I want to be with you."

He didn't return the smile and hers gradually faded away. He reached up and brushed the hair away from her face, caressing it in the process, and looked at her. They remained so for some moments, then she closed her eyes to lean forward and kiss him. She kissed his neck and chest again, then began to discover what parts would make him moan the loudest. Eventually he pulled her back to him and kissed her desperately. When he stopped, she interlaced her fingers with his, his hands flat on either side of his head. She raised her upper body, then lowered herself until they uttered a quiet, simultaneous gasp.

When they had finished, she lay back down on him, still together, enjoying the exquisiteness of it all. She listened to his heartbeat, and felt the slow rise and fall of his chest. Sleep was coming on for both of them, she knew, and that when they awoke, they would be famished. But that was alright. They were together now. And together they could do anything they wanted.

CHAPTER 15

Carrie stood in taupe shorts and a white halter-top, arms crossed, waiting. Torn. Torn between wanting to go, and wanting to stay. Stay and watch him like she had been. Watch him sleeping in her bed, in her bedroom. All hers. She smiled, then looked away almost in embarrassment of how good it felt. It enveloped her in its warmth - she fairly bathed in it, drinking it in, gorging on it. But this had been going on for half an hour now. It was time to go forward. A light stirring from Eben, and she moved to the window and loudly thrust open the curtains.

"Good morning Sunshine!", she sang out to him. "By the time you're up, there will be omelettes for breakfast, er, lunch. Late lunch. Then off for a walk on the beach."

Eben moaned himself to semi-consciousness.

"You mean the same beach that was there yesterday?", he questioned facetiously.

She strode to the bed, grabbed his arm and swung him halfway around. Then she gave him a deep, wet, upside-down kiss. "Yes, but I didn't get to do that on the beach yesterday."

He groaned his acquiescence, and got up to head towards the bathroom. This brought a smacking of his bare bottom. He turned to her in surprise and was met by a mischievous smile.

"I didn't get to do that yesterday either."

Off they went to meander down the beach, south. It was always south. But Carrie no longer questioned it. She was far too happy just being with him. To exult in every moment of it, waking and sleeping. To snuggle up with him as they walked along the sand, his arm around her, with no question of its meaning, both of her arms hugging him in return, like she might never let go. They stopped often to kiss, on impulse, just because, oblivious as to who or what was around them at the time. He placed her on top of a rock, she assumed in order for her to experience what kissing him from above was like, which she obligingly did. Then she jumped on top of him, and somewhat with his help, migrated around him until she was being piggy-backed. Eben saw this as his cue to run full speed into the waves, a foot deep, and Carrie as hers to squeal in mock horror, then to climb to the top of him and cling there in a ball. They teetered like this for a moment, looking like the human equivalent of a lolly-pop, until his strength and balance gave way. After a number of desperate off-balance steps, they came tumbling to the sand in a heap just inland of the water's edge. There they lay for a while, their laughter and heavy breathing gradually dying out. Sadie, welcomed along with no leash, since she could now be trusted to come to her name, and who had been ecstatically barking all the while, arrived to give them each kisses in their turn. Carrie closed her eyes, feeling the waves through the warm sand beneath her back, and blindly searched for Eben's hand to possess. Finally, he spoke.

"So how far can we go before we're out of your County Sheriff benevolent zone?"

"Well, aren't you just Mr. Cynical Rainy Cloud", she teased.

"Oh, come on. They must be dying to get at you. We can't go just anywhere. And look who's talking, Ms. Cynical Glass-Is-Half-Empty," he teased back.

"Those who view the glass as half full may never end up with more than half a glass," she answered, matter-of-factly. "And I'm not cynical. I'm a woman. I'm pragmatic."

This brought a muffled guffaw from the man beside her. She looked up. "And, wherever this limit is, I bet I can beat you to it."

Eben's head popped up for a second, then he was on his feet. But a whimper from her and upraised arms compelled him to help her up also. Whereupon she kissed him, pushed him back to the sand, and took off running with Sadie close behind.

She knew she could keep ahead of him for a while, and determined not to look back in order to maximize her effort. But soon she felt the concussion of his footsteps on the sand behind, and she was in his grasp. His arms clasped around her, he swooped her up and over his shoulders in a sort of fireman's carry, accompanied by her screams of delight. He turned to dash into the waves, and thigh deep, began to raise her up as if to throw her to her fate. An instant terror seized her.

"No Eben! No! Please! No!", she begged. He immediately lowered her down and into his arms, and made his way back to shore. He gently set her down on the beach, and she pressed herself to him, clinging to his neck and burying her face. There he held her as the moments passed.

"I'm sorry", he quietly said. "I wasn't going to...", but the shaking of her head stopped him.

"I'm sorry", she whispered in his ear. "I don't know what happened."

Together, they walked back away from the water to a large rock and sat down against it. Carrie clung on, not wanting to ever let go, not of his warmth, of his tenderness, of his caring. She lifted her head to look into his eyes and was met by a look of depth and wonder.

"I love you", she said.

His face suddenly grew very serious, and he reached up to gently touch her face. After a measured, considered moment, he answered somewhat shyly, "I love you too."

They met in a long, tender kiss, which she broke off to hide her face once again and prevent him from seeing her tears. He didn't seem to notice, but instead stroked her hair and kissed the top of her head. She turned to face the ocean. How contented she felt. In his arms. On her beach. Like she'd been travelling forever to get there. Like everything else had been unimportant. But she perceived that to define it further would require her to remove herself from it, which she wasn't about to do. Instead, she began to search about for something else to focus her thoughts on, and came up with dinner. After a moment, she lifted her head to him in a sweet smile.

"I want to take you out tonight."

Upon reaching the house, Carrie immediately went to make a private telephone call, instructing Eben to dress as chic as possible, and would divulge nothing further. Given the added time needed for she herself to get ready, he was very much at leisure, enough so even to answer the door and accept delivery of the half-dozen red roses in a vase he had ordered for her that morning. He brought them into the bedroom just in time for her to be zipped up, and the, "Oh Eben, they're beautiful! Thank you", plus the kiss he received, seemed more that enough to offset the lack of good timing. Another ring on the intercom, answered and buzzed in by Carrie, and she turned to him with a smile of anticipation.

"I have a surprise for you", she declared, which turned out to be in the courtyard in the form of the funeral car.

"This?", he asked, incredulously.

"Oh yes", she replied. "It's the only way to travel."

A half an hour later they rolled up to a restaurant named "Renato's", and despite the line-up outside were ushered straight in, amongst murmurs and stares. That the commotion wasn't due to their get-into-the-restaurant-free-card, was confirmed once they were inside when the room went suddenly silent, and a hundred or so heads turned towards them as if choreographed to do so. Just then, an older, dapper, pleasant-looking gentleman in a tuxedo, medium height, balding, with a goatee, approached them. Success had come to Renato quite late in life. Carrie had witnessed that a good location, great food, high prices and a taste of normalcy were what the Semi-Glamorous really craved. Renato offered all that, was rewarded as a result, and she was happy for him.

"Miss Carrie", he came forward and bowed. "It has been far, far too long."

"Yes, you are right. It has," she smiled.

"Everything is as you wished. Now enjoy." He reached out for her hand, kissed it, then motioned for the Maitre' D to continue.

As they were led towards the back of the restaurant, a buzz began all around.

"Come, Darling", chimed Carrie, as loud as possible without being ridiculous, and noted the number of cellphones that were suddenly making an appearance.

At the very rear they were given a table which was off by itself near the kitchen, and which, like many others, had the configuration of a very high-backed booth. There were two large glasses of red wine waiting for them, already set out to breathe. The table's obvious characteristic was that no other table in the restaurant had a view of its occupants.

Once seated, Eben took notice. "No menus, I guess", he remarked.

"I think we have time to relax with a little wine, don't you?", she answered, smiling at him, and raising her glass in a toast. "To us", she proposed.

"To us", he replied, and with clinking of glasses they settled into small talk about the restaurant and the weather, driven mostly by Carrie, somewhat trivial for them considering recent events, and with Carrie checking her watch on what seemed like a regular schedule. Within a few minutes there was a general shuffling around the four or five tables to the front of them, which had been empty when they arrived, curiously so considering the line-up outside, as though they were just now being filled.

At length Carrie looked again at her watch, then taking her last sip of wine, and setting down the glass, asked, "Are you ready for dinner?"

Eben gave a bewildered nod, and she nodded in return and signalled to an unknown subject. Within a moment a high, wide cart of pastries, with two burly waiters pushing and pulling it, appeared from the kitchen and began to roll past their table. When it was only just clear, Carrie jumped up, grabbing Eben's hand in the process and pulled him across the aisle, through the kitchen door, past numerous, seemingly indifferent cooks, picked up and handed him a take-out package, and pushed out the rear entrance and into a black van with dark tinted windows. The van started up and began to pull away immediately.

"What's going...".

"No, wait", she cut him off, and with one hand on his arm and the other barely covering a smile, "Wait for the best part".

The van casually exited the alley and circled the block to pull up across the street from the restaurant. Out front was a melee. Dozens of photographers crammed towards the door pushing and shoving each other to be the next inside. Carrie burst into ecstatic laughter, to which Eben joined in. Then she cried out, "Look! There's Borland!"

He indeed could be seen, jumping over and over again on top of the throng as if it would somehow better his chances of getting in, when finally two of his compatriots, tired of his antics, turned and shoved him to the sidewalk, his camera flying though the air.

This increased Carrie's mirth by three times, until tears streamed down her face, and she started to hyperventilate.

"I was...hoping...catch him...inside...bribes...big bill ... so much better! Ha! Ha! Ha! Oh god! Oh god!", she gasped, and stomped her foot several times on the floor.

The hysterics continued until, fearing that long-term health problems might set in, she motioned the driver to continue on, just as the police arrived.

It took several miles and an aching stomach before Carrie managed to regain control. She turned in her seat and gave Eben a huge kiss, then fell back against him, and draped her arms up around his neck. She closed her eyes, allowed her whole body to relax, and let out a big sigh of contentment. Revenge could be sweet, she thought. And with Eben there in her arms, life could be perfect.

CHAPTER 16

Carrie was beginning to lose track of time, which she took as a positive sign. As she lay in bed she had that peculiar sensation of wakening, as from a nap or a night's sleep, in unfamiliar surroundings, when one isn't necessarily afraid, but is unable to perceive exactly where one is. But intuitively she knew she was in her bedroom and had been awake for hours. Still the feeling remained, and she played with it - a sense of removal that had been coming on for some time. Removal from everything but the sweet man beside her. Removal, in particular, from those events before the two of them had come together. It was like looking back over one's shoulder across a beautiful bay at a vast wasteland, now completely shrouded in fog. She knew it was there, but it was such a delicious feeling to enjoy the view with it obscured. She had no wish to travel back through the mist. It was where she needed it to be: buried, and unreachable if she so chose. And it was a choice she knew she would always make. There was a cottage by a river, owned by family friends, where she had spent some of her most precious moments growing up. Eventually it was sold for development and torn down. But she had visited it one last time before the sale, and had never gone back. In her mind it was still there, just as she remembered it. The key was to confine her perception to how she wanted it to be, and let nothing stop her.

She knew it was daytime too, but without any conscious comprehension of it. Rather, she lay watching the soft air gently stir the curtains, and the light through it make playful patterns on the ceiling above. The air was warm without that slightly cool edge of night, and the sound of the surf was less distinct and more muffled by its blending with the muted noise of the distant city. At length she turned to Eben, and watched him softly sleeping for a while. She thought how lovely it was to have him so regularly close at hand, and watched him for a few moments longer. Then it occurred to her that she seemed to be doing a lot of that lately - her the watcher and him the sleeper, and that hardly seemed fair. So she devised for herself a game that she named, "How many kisses to wake Eben." The rules were simple. The kisses had to be light enough so that no one kiss would wake him - it had to be cumulative. And certain areas were out of bounds, including his lips - that would be too direct. She leaned over, quietly pulled back the sheet, and commenced. By three kisses his breathing had lightened, by five he had begun to stir, by eight he was beginning to moan, and by ten she was in his arms.

Carrie laughed and pulled away. "No, you're too easy", she proclaimed, then with an, "Okay, I'll take you anyway", she nestled in against him, and he nestled back.

Her head was on his shoulder, her left hand on his chest, her right in his above the pillows. Her naked body aligned with his, even their toes were inter-twined, and they lay that way for a long time. Every inch of her that was in touch with a corresponding inch of him sent back constant and individual reports of just how delectable it felt. Only his heartbeat and the endless waves marked the passing minutes.

"God this is wonderful", she sighed. "It feels like we're in a bubble. Tell me we won't go back."

"Aren't you forgetting?", he frowned. "Sooner or later we're bound to be invaded."

"No," she whispered, rising to kiss him, then snuggling back into place. "I left a message for Leon to keep cancelling everything one week in advance".

"My you're resourceful."

She gave a slight smile. "I don't want to have to be resourceful anymore." She reached over for his free hand, spent a moment with their palms together, comparing them, then pulled it in to her. "You know, I don't think I ever hated the idea of change before. Until now. Until right this minute." She paused to reflect. "I grew up in South Dakota. My father was a seed agent, but he did some farming on the side. My mother was the dutiful farmer's wife. She's gone now, but he's still there. Won't leave, not even to visit. And I hardly ever go back."

"Do you miss it?"

"No. Not really. I always knew my life wasn't there. But I used to get up every morning before dawn to help my father with the chores. I used to climb up in the barn, sit by the door and watch the sun come up, dreaming of what was going to be. Everything always seemed so full of promise. Freer, somehow. I guess I was different back then. I haven't seen a sunrise for years."

"I know", Eben answered, and she lifted her eyes to his. He opened his mouth to speak, paused for a moment, then went on. "A long time ago a friend of mine and I were driving out west, taking the back roads. We stopped at this little store in the middle of nowhere for some gas. As we were pulling out I saw this farm wagon out by the road, with some sort of produce for sale. There was this young girl, maybe fifteen, sitting on the wagon, leaning back on her hands. She had bare feet, cutoff jeans, a white shirt with the sleeves rolled up, tied around the middle. She looked like it really didn't matter to her if she sold anything, she was just enjoying the day. She had a can of cola in her hand. As we drove out she smiled and raised it to us in a toast. I've never forgotten that image. It was you."

Carrie's mouth was wide open as she stared at him in astonishment. It was a full minute before a word came out, preceded by a slight smile.

"You're fibbing".

He shrugged slightly. "You can believe me or not believe me."

She continued to stare, to try to penetrate those eyes, which betrayed nothing.

"No. You're absolutely fibbing."

This was met by a gentle smile. "It doesn't matter", he concluded, and leaned to kiss her forehead. "Either way, it's true".

Carrie kept up a regular routine of glancing Eben's way, waiting for that moment when, it a fit of hilarity he would break down and admit his story never happened. But it hadn't come. She wondered why she needed that admission. She was honest enough with herself to acknowledge that it could be true, that was, as opposed to being honest with him. But she was a woman, she determined, and had sole custody of those thoughts she chose not to reveal. That she might need it not to be true occurred to her, but she dismissed that question as premature, having not yet settled on the legitimacy of the story in the first place. With that safely out of the way, she could finally settle into anticipation of what was to come.

She looked at him again, his face every few seconds alternately illuminated, then not, by the lights passing by as the funeral car glided on through the night. His face was calm: apparently he was content to await her revealing of the latest surprise she had in store for him on her own time. He looked over at her, smiled mildly, and reached out his hand for hers, which she gladly gave him. She smiled back. This evening was for her as well.

They had been riding a short while to the south but now turned back in the direction of the ocean, travelled through the lights of a residential area, then suddenly plunged into a vast plane of almost total darkness. As they rolled to a stop, little could be seen ahead except a set of elaborate gates. They got out, Carrie in her blue jeans and matching jacket, Eben in his jeans and leather jacket, just as a stocky man stepped through the gates to greet them.

"Mr. Thompson?", she offered.

"Yes. Glad to meet you. Are you ready?"

"Yes. Very", she smiled.

With a nod Mr. Thompson returned back through the gates. Carrie motioned to the driver, and the car disappeared into the blackness, leaving them in silence but for the sound of waves close by, but hidden by the impenetrable dark. She moved closer to Eben, and he wrapped his arms protectively around her. So natural now, she thought. She looked up into his face and could just make out that his fatalistic expression was beginning to give way to bewilderment. She smiled at this, stood on tiptoes to give him a big kiss, and said, "Surprise!"

As if on cue, the whole area behind her began to light up, section by section, with an array of dazzling coloured lights. Shortly, revealed in installments, appeared the sight of the amusement park they had viewed from up the coast, void of life no longer. She could now clearly see Eben's expression - no words came out, but with the wide eyes and open mouth, she knew she had caught him off guard. With a self-satisfied smile, she grabbed his hand and led him, running, through the gates.

The park had existed for many years, so that the layout was the old-time style, wherein the rides were closely-enough arrayed to produce a seemingly endless collage of sight and sound and smell.

"Mmmmm. Onion rings!", declared Carrie, as they began to meander through, taking it all in. Mr. Thompson and his handful of staff had the rides all lit up, and most of them turning, with their different selections of music blaring, so that the only element missing was a throng of other park-goers. That, Carrie didn't miss in the least.

Off they went to the Monster, and the Zipper, and the Holiday Bounce, all of which made Carrie glad they hadn't yet eaten. They tried the Scrambler, before which she was careful to choose the seat wherein she would be the Squisher and not the Squishee. In the House of Mirrors they viewed themselves as a tall, short, wide, narrow, and wavy couple. All good, she proclaimed.

They paused for a veritable feast of burgers, sodas, corn-dogs, and onion rings, topped off with cotton candy and candy apples. They needed something to make the roller-coaster a challenge, she joked.

On to the bumper cars where, without the usual inconvenience of other participants that one had no desire whatsoever to bump, Carrie was free to constantly thwart Eben's strategy of manoeuvring for the best angle, by coming right at him again and again. The "whompf" of the resulting collisions intermixed with torrents of laughter from her, and the crackle of the electric sparks overhead.

Her merriment increased at the House of Glass where it was discovered that, although Eben had successfully navigated himself around the globe, almost, this ability was apparently not transferrable to a small building constructed of transparent material. Carrie had made it through in about forty-five seconds, leaving him behind on purpose, but after four minutes of waiting she decided to go rescue him, somewhat complicated by the fact that the longer he took, the funnier she thought it was, and she was laughing so hard she could barely walk.

At the games of chance, she exhibited that inherent trait of all women to desire in their boyfriends strength, skill, and bravery, except when they are being bested by their one hundred and twenty pound girlfriends. Ring toss, sharp-shooter, water-guns, and basketball throw, she topped him in each. Only at Ring the Bell did he finally prevail, winning for her a stuffed animal of indiscernible parentage, which they decided to name Hank, and which they thought would make a great companion for Sadie.

Off they rolled through the House of Horrors, with Carrie feigning terror at the first skeleton they encountered, which gave her the excuse, not really needed, to snuggle in close to Eben, and commence a long, deep kiss that lasted the duration of the ride and resulted in them not seeing a thing more.

As they strolled along to the ferris wheel, she began her now accustomed habit of embracing Eben, and relying on his support to leave her free to look up and around. She opened herself up to the night and drank it in freely. There was an indescribable feeling to those few, simple moments. Was it magic, she wondered? Was it really so easy to achieve? The wheel came closer, looking impossibly high from her perspective. But they boarded the awaiting car, cuddling together on one side and ignoring the resulting tilt from the absence of anyone on the other. A few butterflies, then off they went, climbing to the height of the arc, circling down through the bottom with a whoosh, then back to the top again. On and on, with no words between them, just looks of contentment and a few quick kisses

Finally the car slowed to stop at the very pinnacle of the wheel. With the carnival sounds far below, Carrie could hear the rushing in of the silence save for the swish of the breeze. Warm but for a tinge of ocean coolness, it freed her hair to toss about in playful gesticulations. She withdrew from Eben just a bit, grabbed hold of the railing, closed her eyes and took a long, slow, breath. She opened them to the sight of the city to her left, where there amassed thousands of endlessly sparking lights, as thick as the stars, she thought, but not. Then to her right, beyond a clearly drawn line, a blanket of infinite nothingness, which she knew to be the ocean, deep, and dark, and empty. But slowly she began to perceive a few specks of light, far out on the horizon. Voyagers on a night sail perhaps, brave enough to venture forth into the void, and now reaping the rewards. She glanced back to the city, then found herself drawn again to the sea. A feeling of serenity began within her, at once all-pervading and at the same time, so lightly borne. She perceptibly relaxed, and for a few moments let the sensation drift through her. She had just commenced to contemplate what might be its source, when the car began to move again.

They strolled towards their last ride, the roller coaster, which she had planned to be so. Carrie's two arms were hugging Eben in affectionate appreciation of all he was, and all she had with him, and she occasionally gave him a sweet glance just to say so. They arrived and boarded their car - it would be first one in the train. She nestled in again, but less closely this time. That two of their hands were grasped together seemed to be enough.

The car lurched forward and she reached over with her free hand, brought Eben's face towards hers, and gave him a momentary kiss. As they started the steep ascent, she looked down to her right to the water's edge, where the incoming surf came alive within the glow of the coaster's lights. She glanced over her shoulder far up the beach to where she knew her home awaited. A less intense, mirror image of the scene she had viewed from the top of the ferris wheel presented itself, but within that she somehow found comfort. She settled back in to complete their journey to the top, and felt a deep, relaxed, satisfaction. At no other place would she want to be, and at no other time. They surmounted the apex, and began to hurtle down the drastic descent. She found herself completely letting go of the outcome. Whatever would happen, it would be wonderful.

The hum of the tires serenaded the quiet of the night. Carrie lay on the back seat with her head on Eben's lap. She was on her side, holding him to her. He had placed his jacket over her shoulders, and was gently caressing her hair. Her eyes were closed - she was exhausted - and knew she would give out long before they reached home. She had enough consciousness for only one thought, but it contented her immensely: that she desired only one thing in life, and here he was, safe in her arms.

CHAPTER 17

Carrie had the superb sensation of having the entire front of her body caressed at once, or was it she caressing him? She drank of him fully, fairly breathing him in, and he her, their bodies together, their beings interminably intertwined. Consciousness returned as a warm mist, and she found them lying as one, her, face down on his back, his naked body held by and in return, supporting hers. How long they had been there, how many moments asleep, the number of times they had made love - these were questions that no longer had purpose in her life. She had known nothing like this - it was like life anew.

She began to softly stroke him and to kiss his neck and shoulders, his back, anything, anything to have contact with him, to taste him. He stirred, then moaned softly. There would be a chance for sleep another time, perhaps even soon. They were totally open to their whims. Wherever this time took them they would travel as though floating on a seemingly endless river. Thoughts beyond this went unnoticed. Were this the culmination of life, then life could end - it would have been worth the journey. She tucked her head around his and began to kiss his lips as best she could, but with a hunger he must have sensed, for he turned, moved on top of her, and kissed her deeply. Their arms and legs wound tightly round each other, desperately they kissed on and on until she clutched the sides of his head in both her hands and lifted her mouth from his. His kisses flowed to other places, and her breathing intensified.

"I can't get close enough to you," she cried almost soundlessly, and their embrace came together powerful and complete.

"I know," he answered quietly.

They held on. Nothing would be rushed now. Everything had its time, as if they thought they had forever. Yet nothing was unimportant, nothing would be wasted, as if they knew it was to end tomorrow. Finally kissing started afresh. They began to slowly revolve until Carrie was on top again and, without thought or effort, they were together. She uttered a light gasp and her eyes closed. But she willed them open to look deep into the grey eyes before her. He was poised there, waiting to gaze into hers. For a long while the look of intensity in his eyes seemed to mirror the almost painful exquisiteness of it all, and which she knew reflected her own. Time and again, with their increasing rhythm, her vision of him slipped away, and she would fight to regain that wonderful perspective, only to once again be drawn from it, away back into herself. Suddenly he raised himself up to meet her and kissed her passionately. It seemed as though an electric current possessed her, like nothing she had ever felt, and she arched back.

"Oh, Eben!", was the response that was not of her conscious making, and she collapsed onto him, surrendering herself completely to his arms, sublimely unable to move or to speak. He kissed her hair, and gently stroked her arms and back, with her softly sighing in return. Finally she lifted her head to his, and gave him a long, delicate kiss, relishing the feel and taste of his lips. They turned onto their sides and, still somewhat intertwined, began to study each other's face from the remote ends of the same pillow. For a while they remained so, sharing a smile of contentment between them.

"I adore you," she whispered to him. He reached up to touch her face in response, and her hand clasped his to hold it in place a moment longer. "Does that worry you?", she asked, a slight mischievous smile appearing on her lips.

"No. Not at all," he replied.

She lifted his hand and kissed it, then, unwilling to relinquish it so soon, brought it in close to her heart. For a moment she fell into deep thought, then frowned seriously.

"You know, that was the strongest orgasm I've ever had."

He replied with a burst of laughter.

"No. Really. That was just . . . wow!"

"Well," he laughed on, "that would explain the adoration".

"Oh! You bum!", she exclaimed, and struck out for that illusive ticklish spot she knew he possessed.

"No! No! Way counter-productive!" He grasped her hand and set about trying to distract her with kisses, until she relaxed once more. He reached to the bedside table for a chocolate truffle which he held just above her mouth, waiting for her tongue to accept the invitation. Out it came, but he allowed it only the slightest of contact, a mere touch of flavour, until she could stand it no more and jumped up to engulf it whole, along with two or three of his fingers. His lips were brought to hers, and they kissed while the morsel dissolved. Chocolate favoured Eben and Carrie, she thought, and smiled.

She kissed away what chocolate was left from his fingers and his face, then lowered her head to his chest, resting there, embracing him, and placing more kisses, thanking him for that little space and for holding her in return. She felt his movement as his arm reached for the radio. In a moment classical music was playing, soulful and tinged with sorrow and life. It resonated within her, yet paradoxically, never had she been so happy. Maybe the two were inseparable, she pondered. Perhaps, in the end, they were indistinguishable. It was sad to think that nothing could ever fully be appreciated unless there was a fear it might be lost.

Quietly she turned from him, slipped off the bed, and tiptoed to the bureau. She picked up a hairbrush and slowly, almost absently, began to run it through her hair. Soon she saw him appear in the mirror before her, and wrap his arms affectionately around her from behind. For long moments her eyes delved into his before her.

"Did you...have you ever thought that, when you look into a mirror", she asked,"you are actually seeing yourself in another dimension, living some sort of other existence?"

"Parallel but different?"

"Yes. Just meeting up at that particular instant."

"Well, I suppose it's possible", he replied.

Carrie studied the image of them for a long while, then queried almost forlornly, "I wonder what will become of them."

He hugged her tenderly, and gave her a tiny kiss on her neck. Then, determined to embrace the moment, she turned, and kissed him on the lips. Her hand grasped his and led him back to bed. She felt a warmth as the rays of the sun descended through the open window and around and onto them. A sunrise or sunset she did not know which. As they settled, she uttered an almost unheard, "Ahhhh". An overwhelming sense of well-being possessed her, and silent tears fell. Quiet sobs followed, prompting Eben to raise his head.

"Are you okay?", he gently asked.

A shaking of her head was immediately corrected by a nodding of her head. "I just need a minute," she answered, between sniffles. He kissed the top of her head, and she held him tightly, allowing herself to fall into letting go of everything. Tears streamed uncontrollably now. A vague yearning to understand it was within her, but the distinction between the advance of the new and the retreat of the old, she was not purvey to. At length, she articulated what amounted to all she knew for sure.

"I'm so sorry."

"Oh, Sweetie", he replied, and brought her up closer to him. "It's . . . it's just that I love you so much."

"And I you."

"It feels like everyone who has come before has existed only to bring me to this moment. More than that. Like I've never ever found my true place before. Until now. Until you."

She wanted to tell him the rest. How she couldn't imagine being apart from him. How she no longer felt whole without him inside her. How, as far more than just sexual, she feared she would never get close enough to him to experience the almost excruciating perfection of their love. That, limited to their emotional, intellectual, and physical connection, their souls would not be permitted to become one. Not in this life. She lifted her head to regain those eyes, his soul, as if the mere thought of her apprehensions might be enough for fate to take him from her in its fickleness.

"I went from nothing to everything with you", he replied. There was a moment shared in silence. "From nothing to gain to everything to lose", he added almost absently. His hand reached up, cupping her face, then lightly tracing down her neck and chest, came to rest upon the small pendant there. He took it in his fingers as though seeing it for the first time.

"It was a gift from Leon," she offered, answering the unasked question.

"White gold?"

"No. He gave it to me when my first album went platinum. "I don't always wear it." She quietly removed it from his grasp, to examine it. Then, suddenly feeling uncomfortable, she returned to it back to its place, but not to him. "Let's not talk about it."

"Hmmm", he half nodded in understanding.

She smiled, and, with a sniff, decided at an instant to lighten the mood. "So, I believe you owe me a story," fixing her gaze on him, with eyebrows raised in expectation.

"A story", he repeated.

"I believe it's called, 'Eben's Other Woman'. You know, the

lovely lady I have to thank for you being here, and now, and mine".
Her eyes began to shine.

"You mean my mother?" The resulting swat compelled him to
try again. He sighed. "A long, long time ago", he commenced and
concluded, appearing to ludicrously expect there was even a remote
chance this might prematurely settle the question.

"Do tell," she invited, with her best effort at a wide-eyed innocent
expression. "We have no secrets. I've seen you naked."

He contemplated for a moment. "Do you honestly believe I'm
going to lie in bed with you and talk about another woman?"

Her extended pout was the sole response proffered, to which Eben
could not help but chuckle. His expression turned sober though, and
after a moment or two replied in a deliberate and measured tone.

"I have come to believe that there is someone in this world for
everyone, but you can't always find them. If you find them, you
can't always make them yours. If you make them yours, you can't
always keep them."

Carrie looked at him, her affectation gone, not so much to study
him, but to absorb the impact of what he had said. Finally, with a
quickly growing smile, she replied, "Well then. We can't waste any
time."

With that, she reached to her side of the bed, where grapes had
been placed on the clear understanding that they would not be
provided peeled, blindly selected one for brevity's sake, and plunked
it into Eben's obediently opening mouth. This shortly resulted in
an, "Mmmm", of approval from him, and another grape from her.
This went on through several more offerings, soon with decidedly
more grapes than, "Mmmm's", until she determined that the "usual"
had become mundane. She began to deposit grape after grape, their
predecessors having little or no time to vacate the space, until a
veritable convention of fruit inhabited his mouth. She leaned back
to admire her accomplishment, and the sight of his face, puffed up
like a chipmunk's, launched her into very poorly disguised mirth.
After several moments if gulping down grapes which she suspected

were, out of sheer necessity, mostly whole, he emerged unscathed and with a smile.

"I hope at least those were seedless," he admonished.

"Seedless?", she responded with as straight a face as she could muster. "They make those?"

The resulting look of audacity on his face caused her to lose all control and she fell back on the bed, her silvery peals of laughter filling the room. At once he seized the opportunity and was on her to gain the advantage and turn her on his knee. Knowing she could not give in, she squirmed and struggled, and squealed in delight. At last, due to her already weakened state, she relented, and her whole body relaxed.

"Go ahead, you brutish man!", she teased. "Have your way with me!"

To this he feigned to strike, declaring, "This is going to hurt me more than it is you," then stopped short, and bent down to gently nibble her bare bottom, followed by a kiss.

"What, that's it? You're fired! Next!", she called out, and then doubled up in convulsions of laughter.

He immediately targeted her ticklish areas, of which there were many, until they collapsed together in a fit of hilarity.

Bit by bit they recovered, which was followed by many kisses of any spot that availed itself to that end. Ultimately, though, it was their lips that were sought after, and they were re-claimed, their hands rejoined above their heads, and he rolled on top of her. She welcomed the weight and feel of him, and enveloped him with her legs, urging him to her. She held her breath as he moved forward, the life flowing through her again only when he had returned to her once more. His kisses gently fell in a hundred places, and she was nurtured by them as in a soft rain. His hands moved behind her back to her shoulders now, and he raised himself up. She grasped him by the hips. To possess him mind, body and soul could not be by any one more than any other, and would not be any less.

She watched him intently as his movement gradually increased in speed, his gaze never leaving hers. Through the sheer intensity of emotion and feeling she had time for only fleeting thoughts. That this could not possibly be of this world. That they had been borne beyond their existence to a sublime reality which, moment by moment, was of their own fantastic creation. And that it was only as pure and divine a combining of two souls as this, that marriage was truly meant to sanctify.

They continued on for several moments more when Eben's body became taut, his eyes grew in intensity, and he uttered a soundless cry. She felt him anew, and as he settled into her arms they shared one, final, exquisite kiss, before drifting into a state of enhanced and exalted sleep.

CHAPTER 18

Carrie became conscious in a state of neither sleep nor wakefulness. Like one of those early morning dreams, she thought, the ones that cling to you even after the light's been turned on in an attempt to establish their status as mere dreams. This seemed different, however. And she had no conviction whatsoever of the hour.

The process of thought accompanied her in this dream, if that's what it was, but it felt detached and remote from her surroundings. The memory of Eben came to her, but in an abstract way. Her normal choice would have been to slide over to cuddle and maybe even kiss, but she knew somehow obliquely that was not going to occur. She inferred that he must be beside her in bed only through the sole rationale that she had no reason to suppose he was not. And a certainty possessed her that this faith was all that she was to be permitted for now.

She lay there for some time, almost transfixed in the moment, not moving, peering at the mostly darkened room, or at least as much as her position afforded her. The air was still and heavy - no sounds came from outside. A dream where nothing happens, she pondered. That's different. Finally she commenced to perform the only course seemingly within her power. But even the act of rising proved difficult. It took many moments of deliberate concentration before movement began, and even then it was as if in slow motion.

Eventually she was on her feet, swaying somewhat unsteadily as she waited to establish some measure of balance. As she did so, she began to move sluggishly, but almost pre-determinably, to where she had left her shorts and t-shirt on the floor. Just when she could not precisely recall. She felt their cool presence as they went on her, then she noted her gradual progress towards the door. Good idea, she figured. Get out. Clear your head.

Carried felt herself round the corner and start down the hallway, which for some reason seemed incredibly long. But she determined that she was moving, she observed, as the light began to strengthen at every measured step. As it did, she noticed the air. It was all around her, thick as in the bedroom but now increasingly visible. She marvelled at its form, like a translucent fog, and could feel it as it passed by, warm and enveloping, like walking under water. By the time she reached the landing, all wondering about her destination had ceased. She was satisfied in this moment, in this reality, and a heightened sense of contentedness possessed her. It was not to be compared with that of her closeness to Eben, for it seemed separate and of a different sort, though somehow innately connected.

She gained the landing and was instantly overwhelmed by the view it afforded. The glass door and wall of windows before her were overflowing with a brilliant golden light, the illumination defused but by no means diminished by the denseness of the air that carried it to her. She sensed her movement towards it, all questions of purpose forgotten, replaced by a curiosity and fascination that she would follow in complete trust.

Carrie continued on, drifting through the door and onto the deck, when a sudden feeling of complete detachment pervaded her. In astonishment, she began to recede from the image of herself, to then follow her path to the first chair she came across that faced the light. She sat down, and almost imperceptibly began to settle back into her form once again. An extreme haze gave a whitewashing of all that was before her, the ocean and sky, but in its centre lay the incredible brilliance of the sun, obscured and unfocused, but no less powerful. Its position halfway concealed below the edge of the sea signalled that this day was nearly done. Bathed in warmth and softly caressed by it, Carrie felt liberated from all stress, all cares, from the weight of all that possessed her. She vaguely found herself surveying what lay before her. She noted the shapes of several people, dark and somewhat grainy, she thought, moving slowly about at different points on the beach. It was then that it began to be revealed to her that the scene she was viewing was completely devoid of sound. No crashes of waves, no cries of seagulls, no chattering of humans, no sound of the wind, if there was any to be heard. She felt truly as though she were in a vacuum, having no power to perceive, much less change, what might be ahead, but only to observe and wait to emerge anew.

Carrie's glance took her a long way up the beach, where something drew her attention. It was almost indistinguishable at first, but the longer she looked, the more it began to define itself. Three figures were there. Three boys, it appeared, the indistinctiveness of each accentuated by the shadow which the setting sun caused him to be. They were huddled around three sides of a large hole they were digging in the sand. The boy in the centre was kneeling upright at its edge, the boy on the left sitting with his legs dropped over one side, the boy on the right sprawling flat, peering over the rim. She studied the image for a long time, as she floated high up on her deck, but could find no inclination to define it. It could not be done. It was clear, simple, and exquisite action without purpose, and she revelled in beholding it, for their sakes and for hers.

She turned back to the sun and as she did so, caught a minute glimpse of a runner up the beach, coming from the direction of the boys. Again, the shadow he bore made the figure as hazy as the sky itself, but she somehow instinctively knew him to be a man. He had the power of the athletic male, but there was in his stride a certain fluidity that made her unable to turn away.

And then she was with him, a little ways behind, but matching him stride for stride in a state of shared grace. On and on they ran, and she began to experience an incredibly heightened feeling of almost effortless motion. She fairly flew down the beach, unaware of her steps, only that the air had suddenly become fresh and alive. A brilliant flash of yellow drew her attention to her right, where the last of the sun dove beneath the horizon, only to instantly emerge in an outburst of golden light into the sky.

Carrie felt her heart rise and she surged forward. The runner was no longer there, moved ahead or fallen behind, she did not know or care. Never before had she felt so free, so euphoric, so ecstatically alive. For a few further moments she drank it in, feeling it all around and within her. Then with no break in her speed she veered sharply to her right, plunged headlong into the ocean, and disappeared.

CHAPTER 19

Carrie surveyed the room about her. Not much else to do. Long and low, with a bank of windows on one side overlooking the comings and goings as they came and went. Strangely vacant, opulent, expensive and uncomfortable, with an odd combination of metal and organic rust-coloured furnishings in the latest style. If the public only knew where its money went. A mountain of fresh fruit with available yogurt dip on one table, a forest of beverages on another. She wondered what would become of it all. She wasn't hungry, at least not enough to eat a mountain. Just bored. Well, it was an airport, after all. The VIP Lounge no less. Sounds like something from a strip club, she mused. Still, that explained the scarcity of passengers. It was a commuter-sized jet, though still a commercial flight. Nobody had private jets anymore, except maybe nineteen year old pop stars who were too stupid to care where their money went, or who didn't expect to make it to twenty.

God, I'm a grump, she reflected. The stress of a journey coming to an end, combined with a feeling of being in the cross-hairs. But she felt she could put up with people for a few hours more. The flight was expensive enough that those who could afford it wouldn't be a bother. They would rather die than acknowledge that anyone could be so much more important so as to deserve their notice. And they were the limo to the tarmac crowd - far too busy to idle away precious time in a VIP Lounge. As for her, this was one flight she wasn't about to risk a driver not being on time for.

She turned her view to where Eben was standing, studying the fruitscape, seemingly attempting to fathom its deep, inner mysteries. Solitary as a pineapple, and just as uncommunicative. Carrie stole up behind him and quietly wrapped him in her arms. She closed her eyes, and for a long while held him, feeling his warmth, loving that he was there.

"My Love", she declared.

He did not respond, but gently laid his hand upon hers. After a brief time filled with unspoken words, she continued.

"You're thinking."

For a moment longer he remained silent, apparently thinking still. Then he replied, "I still don't understand."

She put her hands on his hips and effortlessly turned him to face her. She looked into his beautiful eyes, and placed her hand to the side of his cheek, as if to hold them there forever.

"I don't understand why you have to do this," he continued, his eyes moving away from the confines of her hand.

"I told you. It's something I need to do."

"But for weeks you've been hiding away...."

"Recreating."

"...recreating away. Why this?"

Her shoulders shrugged. I can't keep things open-ended forever. It's time to set things straight. And I trust him."

"What will you say?"

"I...I don't really know yet."

"But you don't want me with you."

She closed her eyes slightly and smiled just a bit. She moved to face Eben, and to embrace him.

"You know I would love for you to come. But it has to be just me. Please understand."

He studied her briefly, then his face relaxed. He nodded perceptibly and gave her a half-smile of his own.

"When I get back, let's go somewhere", she offered. "Anywhere. As far as we want for as long as we want."

"Reality will always catch up with you."

She smiled at him. "Do you really think I don't have money elsewhere?"

"That's not what I meant", he replied.

"Miss Ralston?", a voice advancing up the hallway called out.

Carrie's head turned slightly in the direction of the sound, then returned to Eben.

"Miss Ralston?", called the voice again.

"I'll be back tomorrow. I love you so much!", she declared, giving him a quick but deep kiss.

"I love you too", he returned as she receded from him, and their grasping arms stretched out and finally parted. With a wave made as light as she could manage, she turned a corner to follow the guide.

"Ready in five minutes", said the voice.

Carrie remembered that phrase from not too long before. She couldn't precisely recall when, but she knew it hadn't been good.

The light emitting from an extremely large television created its own island of truth, affecting only that which it reached and leaving all else shrouded in relative darkness. Everything it encompassed unavoidably became a smeared, ever-mutating projection of whatever was represented on the screen. Contained within its sphere was a small collection of livingroom furniture, trendy, although not overly expensive, and the figure of Eben, sitting very upright, hands on his knees, at one extreme end of the sofa. He was dressed casually but nice, in khakis and a buttoned shirt, and remained expressionless through a seemingly endless series of commercials. Finally there was music and applause, and then a generic talk show set. As the applause died away, the host, a middle-aged man with greying hair, began to speak.

"Our next guest is a great friend of our show. As you know, she has risen to the top of the music industry in a very short time, and we are so glad to have her back. Please welcome, Carrie Ralston."

Carrie entered from the left, wearing a simple, knee-length, ivory-coloured dress and matching high heels. As she gave a small wave and a smile of relaxed contentment, the audience rose to give her an ovation, reserved, but heart-felt. For an instant she slowed her step, the smile becoming less sure, then shyly hastened on to the host. He, she embraced and offered a quick kiss on the cheek, before waiving again, and taking the closest chair. When the applause died, she reached up to wipe away a small tear.

"How are you, Carrie?"

"I've never been better. How are you?", she replied with a smile, and put her hand briefly on his arm.

The host looked somewhat taken aback.

"Well, I'm fine thank you. And you...you've been the subject of a lot of press stories lately, that I'm sure most of the audience is aware of. A lot of stories detailing concert problems and conflicts with your label. And you've decided to give only this one interview."

"Yes, that's right." She took a deep breath. "My first national interview was on New York Live."

"Well, we're always happy to see you. And, like a lot of your fans, we've been wondering...."

"Listen, Robert", she interrupted, placing her hand on his arm again. "I really appreciate your having me on, but I came here to announce just one thing." Her eyes briefly scanned the faces before her. "That, effective immediately, I am permanently quitting music."

During the prolonged silence that followed, Eben sat emotionless before the screen. Behind him, quietly emerging into the glare, appeared the figure of Melanie, dressed in a cocktail dress, with no shoes, carrying two glasses of champagne. She seemed transfixed by the television, her mouth slightly open, her expression somewhat blank.

Finally the host recovered. "I know you've had some issues...but surely there are solutions with your label."

Carrie smiled slightly, and looked off for a moment in mild contemplation at nothing in particular. "I can only say that Hank Hendriek is the most arrogant, corrupt asshole that I have ever known."

A collective gasp washed over her and was gone. She took the opportunity to shift forward as if to leave, but suddenly halted. "I would like to say...to my fans...I would like to say I'm...." She glanced around the room one final time. "Thank you. With all my heart." With that, Carrie quietly rose and disappeared the way she had come.

Eben, too, stood, then began to move towards the door, when he noticed Melanie. His mouth dropped slightly, and his eyebrows raised.

"I...I thought we were going to celebrate, you know...", she entreated.

He pondered her for a very brief second. "I'm sorry, I shouldn't have come."

She studied him in return, but little time was needed. "You do", she declared, mournfully. "Don't you."

Eben paused long enough that his eyes dropped his vision from her, then noiselessly left through the door.

In retrospect, maybe taking the first plane back after her appearance wasn't the best of ideas. She had only one chance to try to phone Eben, and he didn't pick up. And very little of the past five hours had actually involved any sleep. Instead, Carrie had ineffectually attempted to gain at least some rest through closing her eyes every once in a while. Oh well, she thought. Plenty of opportunity for that later.

She spent scarcely any time in thinking of the show. It was like the last page of the last chapter of a book - she was eager to move on to the next. And she had no desire to speculate what it might involve. She and Eben would fill that in together. It would contain anything they wished, and as it would be theirs alone, it would be exquisite.

Still, she couldn't quite escape a certain heady feeling. She stood almost in awe on the brink of a dream fulfilled, one almost unimagined a few months before, but one felt so strongly it surely had a connection deep within her soul. In some ways it was beyond her to grasp the reality of it - to appreciate all that it truly meant. How long had she been imprisoned in a life of her own making, where a home, security, the latest trends, and trendier friends meant everything? Like every other woman she knew, she had consistently run from any possibility of a love even remotely as deep as that which she had with Eben.

She had no answer, so instead turned to replaying in her mind their last kiss together at the airport. It was the last kiss before the first kiss of the rest of her life, she smiled to herself. She pondered last kisses, how some were known to be so at the time, while so many others could never be anticipated, and only known to be so in retrospect. The sadness of that idea began to permeate her, and she wondered if all women, as soon as they finally found what meant most to them, immediately feared that it would suddenly be taken away.

The announcement of the plane's initial descent interrupted her thoughts, and she quickly returned her seat to its upright position, as though the speed of her reaction might somehow hasten the landing. A red glow out of her window caught her eye, and she watched the reflected rays of the rising sun behind her grow in intensity on the wing. She strained in her seat, but could not view its source, so she had to content herself with watching as its radiance carried her homeward. Carrie could not remember that last time she had experienced a sunrise, but made a heartfelt promise to herself to do so soon.

CHAPTER 20

Carrie entered her front door in complete silence, and not to keep from waking Eben. It was an innate fear, wholly within her, one that grew with each successive mile from the airport, she forcing bill upon bill on the driver, and begging him again and again to hurry. It was an agonizing, all-prevailing certitude that, no matter how deeply and completely she knew her love and life with Eben to be, it would not be allowed to take form in a future reality. Try as she might she could not travel there in her mind and soul. It was an instinct that caused her first step to be down the hallway to check for his knapsack, but it wasn't needed. Out of the corner of her eye she spotted it propped up against the wall in the livingroom, just as it had been that day they first met, that day that seemed so long ago.

Thoughts streamed through her mind - she didn't have to seek them out. She had always known he might leave, expected it almost, but in a way that was almost theoretical, like the chances of contracting some dread disease. She couldn't comprehend it, now that it had come. How something so beautiful could flourish one moment and be so utterly lost the next. Could he not see it? The question of the veracity of their love was one that she did not examine. There was no need, for she had never been more sure of anything in her life.

She knew where he would be. Quietly she set her travel bag down, but could make no further move. It was like she was frozen in a physical manifestation of a line of time. In her moment, she and Eben were in love - all that they could imagine was theirs. Their souls had been intertwined, but they had barely begun. She could smell him, taste him, hear him, talk to him, feel his presence within her still.

Before her lay another dimension, another time which she could see but not approach, although only a trifling distance ahead. She could not enter it, because she would not enter it. She could not accept a reality in which her love meant nothing, for to do so would be to forsake belief in all things. Her eyes closed, and for a few brief moments she found herself relaxing, floating almost, drinking in a warm bath of what it was to be them, holding onto it and letting it softly caress her in return, embracing the loveliness of it one last time. God, could he not feel it?

Her movement forward was not one that would ever be explained, perhaps any more so than the passage of time itself. With every step she felt it so, the contracting of her heart, the tightening of her throat, the all-encompassing physical pain, the breath that had abandoned her. Irretrievably, she stepped onward, silent and slow, accompanied by one solitary tear, until she came upon his form. He was sitting in a deck chair, bent forward with his elbows on his knees, his fingers clasped together haphazardly, seeming to stare at all of them and none of them. He noticed her presence, for his vision looked partially in her direction, but did not address her fully. For a long time nothing was said between them - each knowing that the other knew as well. Finally, it was she who spoke, quietly, almost imperceptibly.

"I don't understand."

Eben's mouth parted slightly, but it was many moments before words came forth, words she was sure were coming.

"I have to leave."

That it failed to satisfy her was clear. And she knew somehow that he could not fail to comprehend this. But to pursue it further was not, for her, as of right or out of principle. She simply understood that she would not survive not knowing why.

"Did something happen?", she asked.

This brought a barely perceptible shaking of his head. This was followed by several moments of silence, then her voice, tiny and far away.

"What did I do wrong?"

He turned from her momentarily, and when he looked back she could see his eyes were wet. He shook his head again, but more vehemently.

Carrie stood before him, arms at her side, unguarded and exposed. But it was what she wanted. To be vulnerable at that moment did not matter. The pain could not touch her in any event, not when she would gladly endure it to not have him leave. Nothing that could be conceived of could possibly affect her as deeply. So she would let it in - it would become one with her. Finally he went on, hesitantly.

"I can't...be what you want me to be." He spoke to her peripherally, grasping his temples in his hands. "That's too much responsibility."

She brought her hands to her front, clasping one little finger within the fingers of the other hand.

"But I love you," she offered. "When...when you're in love, you... you want it all." She turned her tears to the sea. "The touching...the giving...." She looked down, and in a whisper she did not know that he heard, "You crave the chance to be everything."

She returned her view to him, but his countenance had not changed. She searched her being for something, anything to convince him, to make him realize. Yet it was not desperation that compelled her next words, but a need, deep within her, a longing to meet with him in the realm of pure, exalted truth.

"Don't you see?"

His face betrayed neither comprehension, nor its lack. For uncounted moments he remained in seeming contemplation, until finally he rose and faced her.

"I can't be a life to you."

She saw him move past her in a disjointed stream of images. He returned having retrieved the knapsack, and briefly paused by her side. Through a voice, almost inaudible, the words, "Forgive me", came to her.

Further he went, on to the stairs, began to descend, and was gone.

For interminable moments Carrie stared into the void that had been left by his going. Then, as if by compulsion alone, she vaulted forward and started down the steps, decidedly, but haphazardly in her haste, missing the last two entirely. She threw off her sandals, while simultaneously scanning the beach in both directions. But that was not required. There was only one direction he would be.

She raced halfway to the water and peered towards the south. It was a strikingly clear morning, with the sun just completing its rise, blazing down upon her, and she had to use her hand to shield her eyes from its glare. Far off in the distance, farther than she would have anticipated, was the figure of Eben. Eben moving slowly, but with a curious steadiness. Eben moving away from her. He was such a distance, she did not know how she knew him to be Eben at all.

Still he walked on, he is his present and future, leaving Carrie behind in hers, the expanse between them vast and insurmountable. She felt herself give out and softly sink to her knees on the sand. Her eyes flooded with tears as she watched his form gradually diminish, then disappear. Isolated and alone on that long stretch of beach, words came to her lips, barely perceptible, but essential, and which would not be denied.

"But I need you."

EPILOGUE

The man walked on the beach, neither assimilated in, nor an obstacle to, the effluence of the setting sun. He had commenced his walk much earlier in the day. As the sun began to rise, it had paused to lavish its genial warmth upon him from the midst of a vast, cerulean sky.

He walked on, red knapsack slung over his shoulder, a pace unto himself while the world around him hurried by, with an as yet undying steadiness. In some places the border to his left reflected the development of man. Some, perhaps little known, where the presence of man could scarcely be felt. Rocks gradually gave way to palms and shallow dunes, and to his right, the ocean. Always.

The sand became a roadway, desert-rimmed, with far off continuous low and level peaks of clay red, their hue transmuting to one more of green with every succeeding step; the desert metamorphosizing to scrub-grass, ultimately overtaking the mountains and everything else in its path; large and ancient oak trees growing up with Spanish moss descending from their limbs; evolving into semi-tropical foliage, threatening to close in all about and above; then falling back to the quiet of marshland and sun-infused rivers; rocks drawing up again, sprouting pines and mountains; then mellowing into rolling hills and valleys of myriad greens.

In a seaside town the pre-dawn darkness was broken by light from a doorway, which opened onto a deck adorning the second story of a small, grey-clad, wooden building. The man emerged, paused to sling his knapsack onto his shoulders, then began to descend the stairway. Before he reached the bottom, a woman, middle-aged with reddish hair, appeared from the door he had vacated. She watched him, but made no effort to call out or follow. When he gained the street and disappeared from view, she quietly went back inside, and surrendered the door to the darkness again.

Down the road the man travelled, through the ebbing and flowing of farmland, the brilliant colourful splashing of trees, and cool embracing by the rain. One evening he reached the main street of a village, one seemingly stolen from a picture-postcard, with its immaculate store-fronts amongst mature trees and ornate benches and streetlights. In the stillness of the crisp evening, and with an occasional snowflake floating down upon him, he stopped to kneel and search through his knapsack. He seemed to take no notice of the building behind him, two storey, granite block, its outline from the view of its front tapering downward in angles and curves, perhaps once a carriage house. No notice of the sign at its peak reading, "The Little Theatre", or of a playbill posted by its wide wooden doors:

THE LITTLE THEATRE PRESENTS:
CARRIE RALSTON
Her Songs - Her Voice
November 8th - 7:00pm - $15.00

No notice of the sound of a quiet, solitary guitar, uncertainly played, that had been drifting through the doors, slightly open to the night air, the words it carried past him, or the female voice from whom they came. Her voice was flowing and full: sometimes intense, sometimes mellow, but always clear and expressive. She worked with the guitar to create an emotion-charged melody:

> What words can last a lifetime,
> What true loves' final kiss,
> What embrace can prove a lifeline,
> In truth, there are none like this.
>
> When last we viewed the mirror,
> Those in that other place,
> On much different journeys disappeared,
> With our own they left us faced,
>
> I will remember this and you,
> And dream of us in vain,
> Farewell my love, and remember too,
> The love that shall remain.

The man slowly rose, placed the knapsack over his shoulders, and carried on, leaving the sounds behind him in the night.

Still the man moved on, though vineyards silent with frost rising up and over and amidst; then among the limitless structures of man, overwhelming and engulfing, but which saw fit to release him apparently by reason only of his seeming insignificance; then down a lonely country road, perhaps recently surrounded by farm fields, but now more akin to desolate tundra, two feet deep in early morning snow.

For some time, ahead of him in the stillness, lay the glow of a few lights. They gradually began to form part of a small town, but even combined, they did nothing to warm the frigid winter air. He approached the outskirts of the town just as a strengthening sun began to rise above the distant horizon, the vast white cloaking between thrusting though the remaining darkness.

At one of the first, small, wartime homes, the figure of a second man could be distantly seen. He was large and bear-like, and a regular scraping resonated as he toiled to remove the offending snow from his driveway. He wore just rubber boots, sweat pants and a t-shirt, yet the perspiration poured from him, and his face was the colour of his light red hair. He glanced at the man approaching, but did not pause in his battle, until a second, sustained look caused him to halt completely. He straightened and leaned on the top of his shovel, breathing heavily for a moment.

"Son of a bitch", he declared.

The approaching man walked further up the street, and turned into the partially cleared driveway and the waiting massive arms.

"Jeez it's good to see you", the big man proclaimed. Then, after a moment, "Why didn't you tell us?"

The smaller man shrugged. "I don't know. I guess I didn't know what to say."

"Five years is a damned long time. Well, you're home anyway. Come on in. Your sister's up - she'll be glad to see you. And we left your room just the way it was." And in response to the sympathetic, questioning look, "No. We tried, but it just was never going to happen, I guess. Come on. We'll go over to your folks' later. They're pretty much over it all, even the name thing." He smiled, and with an affectionate whack on the back, the walking man was led into the house.

The room was small and sparsely furnished with a single bed, dresser and bedside table, and few adornments on the walls, but had been kept neat and clean. The window was fitted out with vertical blinds, almost closed, so that the glare of the rising sun cast sharp lines along the opposite wall, in the centre of which was the bedroom door. The door opened and the walking man entered, just a few feet at first, pausing, as if feeling its impact once again. He walked to the bed, layed his knapsack down, and continued to the window.

He deftly pulled the cord, drawing the blinds completely and letting the light pour in. Standing there for a few moments, he allowed it to flow over him.

Then he breathed in deeply, and turned back to the knapsack. He bent over to open one compartment, resulting in a cascade of shells and stones and other keepsakes. Out of the midst of the pile he drew several small items, unwrapped but presumably meant as gifts, and made his way to the door. Noticeably left behind was a silver-coloured pendant. It was a simple, tiny, rectangular piece on the end of a very fine chain, but it glistened furiously in the sunlight. The man departed, leaving the room to bathe in the glow of the sunrise, unadulterated and unconstrained, as did, to the right of the door, on the wall, the image of Carrie Ralston.